Escape from Castle Ravenloft

HALT, ADVENTURER, AND READ THESE WORDS BEFORE YOU PROCEED!

You are about to embark on a journey. To where, only you could possibly say. It is not a journey like any you have been on before, where you start at page one and continue on a straight course until you reach the end. Instead, you will be presented with many choices along the way. Each time you are faced with one such choice, make your decision from the options given and then follow the directions to continue your adventure. Once your quest has come to an end, either favorably or, as I'm afraid in some instances it is foretold to, gruesomely, return to the beginning or the last choice and try again.

This is not a journey for those who prefer to sit back and let others make the tricky decisions. This is a journey for a leader, a true hero. One who is not afraid to face off against vampires, stand against zombies, or battle with werewolves. If this doesn't sound like you, turn back now and forget you ever came this way. But if this whiff of adventure has whet your appetite, then forward with you, my friend. And good luck!

DUNGEONS & DRAGONS

ENDLESS QUEST

ESCAPE FROM CASTLE RAVENLOFT

MATT FORBECK

You wake in a large four-poster bed in a musty room that smells of cold stone and ancient death. As you look out a wide window, you witness the last glow of the setting sun muffled behind thick clouds as it fades away, leaving darkness to take the sky.

Where are you, and how did you get here? The last you remember, you were leaving the town of Daggerford after presiding over evening services as a cleric of Tyr, the god of justice, part of an outreach effort you've been making from your nearby home of Waterdeep. As you'd set out on the road, a thick fog enveloped you, making it almost impossible to see past your horse's nose.

Maybe you should have turned back, but you could barely see the road in any direction. You stopped as you pondered your predicament, and that's when you saw a pair of glowing red eyes emerge from the shrouding blackness.

You sit up in the bed, throwing off the sheer black sheets and thick blankets. Thankfully, you're fully clothed, although in an old-fashioned and high-collared outfit you don't recognize. Your armor and weapons are missing.

Your hand goes to your throat, and you find you're still wearing your necklace. It bears the holy symbol of your chosen god, Tyr. The familiar feel of it gives you comfort, and you breathe a tentative sigh of relief.

Your breath catches in your chest, though, when you realize that you're not alone.

A haughty man with jet-black hair and pale white skin tinged with blue steps out from the shadows. He's dressed in an exquisite black cloak lined with crimson silk, layered over a pristine white shirt and coal-black pants. He wears his ebony hair slicked back from his wide forehead in a sharp widow's peak and tucked behind his pointed ears.

He's not breathing.

You instantly recognize his eyes, which glow with a hellish hue. You last saw them on the road to Waterdeep.

He bares his teeth in what he may believe is a welcoming smile. The pointiness of his canine teeth, though, shoots a shudder down your spine.

He can only be a vampire.

"I am Count Strahd von Zarovich," he says with the accent of an ancient aristocrat. "Welcome to Castle Ravenloft. Your new home."

You steady your voice before you reply. "I don't mean to seem ungrateful," you inform him, "but this isn't my home."

The count smiles again. "It may take time to adjust, but you'll come to love Ravenloft once you've been fully recruited. All members of my court do."

You stand up to defy the wicked creature. "I've no interest in joining your court—nor in spending another moment here."

Strahd chuckles. "Time has a way of changing minds, and I have as much time as I like."

He gives you a shallow bow and makes for the door. "I leave you to your own devices. While you may be my guest here, I ask you to confine yourself to this room and the lounge next to it—for your own safety. Also, please remember this. My time on this world may be unlimited, but my patience with those who disrespect my hospitality isn't."

As the vampire lord strides out the door, you contemplate your options. Perhaps it would be better to confront him now, but he exudes so much power, you worry that not even Tyr could protect you.

Climb out the window. Turn to page 6 . . .

Attack Strahd. Turn to page 8 . . .

Escape through the door. Turn to page 16 . . .

You swing at the werewolf with your hammer, but it ducks and tears into you with its vicious claws. Pray to Tyr for help as you might, you do so in vain.

Some unknown time later, you wake to find yourself lying by a fire at the edge of a wolf's den. A rough-and-tumble man with a bushy black beard grunts at you as you rise. You check yourself for the wounds you were sure would kill you, but find nothing except nearly healed scars on your skin.

"How long was I out?" you ask.

"Almost a month," the man says in a gruff voice. "It's easier that way."

"Easier for whom?"

The man points toward a distant line of mountains in the east, and you see a brand-new full moon rising there.

"Would you rather spend a month wondering what's going to happen to you?" the man asks. "Or would you rather just get right down to it?"

You open your mouth to ask him what he means, and why he seems to be growing hairier by the second, but you are distracted when your face

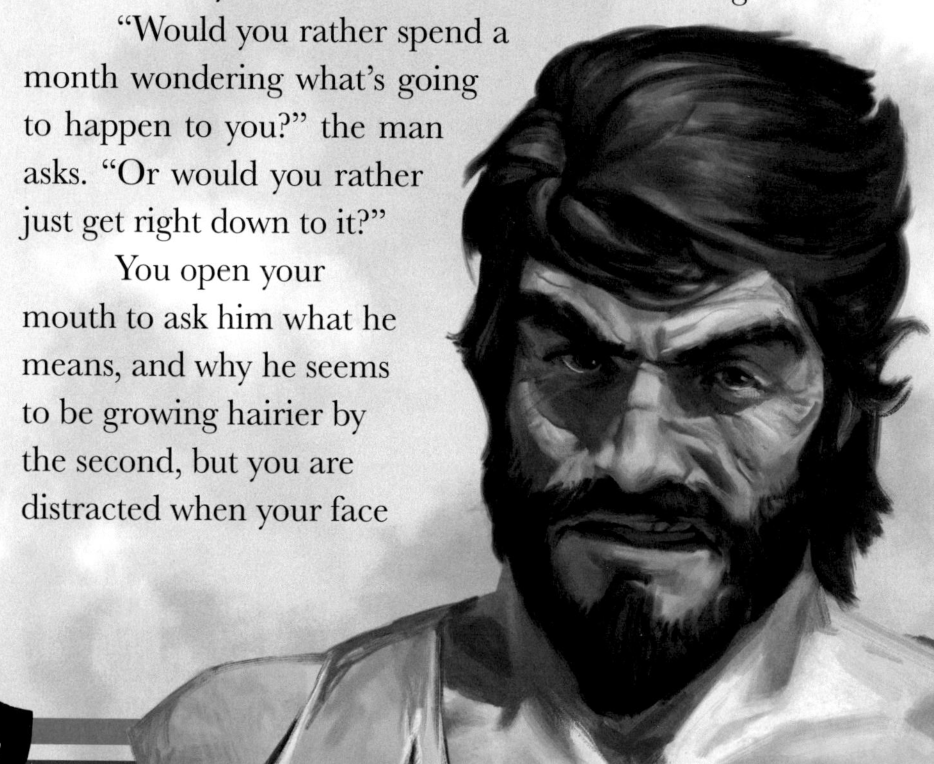

starts stretching out into a fang-filled snout and your hands turn to claw-tipped paws.

You try to shout in protest, but the only thing that comes out is a mournful howl.

It's time for your first hunt to begin.

THE END

As soon as Strahd leaves the room, you turn toward the window, open it, and stick your head out into the chilly air. It's a long drop down to the courtyard below, which is barely visible through the silvery, night-shrouded mist, but you can't stay here.

Under other circumstances, you wouldn't risk the climb down from such a precarious position, but to remain here to await the count's mercy seems like a path toward certain death. Better to risk death now than face the surety of it in the future. You swing yourself over the window's ledge and work your way down toward some nearby climbing vines that offer you a better purchase on the tower's mist-slicked sides.

After taking a moment to steel yourself, you lower yourself into the courtyard that surrounds the castle as quickly as you can manage. There's a terrifying moment when your hand slips and you nearly plunge to your death, but soon enough you're on the cobblestone-paved ground. You survey the area and see that, while you might have escaped the tower in which you were trapped, you're still a long way from free. A wall of cut stone rings the courtyard in which you stand. It's almost as tall as the castle itself, not only protecting the place from potential invaders, but also keeping you from fleeing.

There's an open archway in the protective wall to your right and you make for it, moving as silently as you can. As you emerge through the archway and into the castle's front courtyard, the howl of a wolf echoes through the night. Another responds to it, and then another.

Through the mist, you see two pairs of hungry eyes staring at you, the light of the full moon reflecting in their pupils. You glance back toward the arch you just came through, and you see another three pairs of eyes following you.

Run! Turn to page 12 . . .
Fight! Turn to page 14 . . .

As Strahd strolls away from you, you leap for the door creaking closed behind him and jam your foot in it. He spins about and blinks at you, confused for a moment at what you're trying to do.

You grab the holy symbol from around your neck, shove open the door, and thrust the symbol into his face. "Back, you foul beast!" you shout at him. "The holy power of Tyr compels you!"

Slowly, the edges of his lips curl up into a cruel smile.

"Perhaps you would care to rephrase that?" He cocks a pointed ear toward you as if he couldn't possibly have heard you right.

You suppress a gasp of surprise at how little Strahd seems to care about your demands, and you hold your holy symbol steady before you, out at your full arm's length. You pray with all your might that Tyr will lend you what strength you need to defeat the vampire. Worshipping your god has gotten you this far in life, after all, and you put your trust in your unshakable faith that he won't ignore you now.

"Get back, you undead monster! You're an atrocity! Your very existence is an offense to the living."

Strahd is unmoved. "Now, this," he says, "is exactly the kind of disrespect I was talking about. What kind of a guest treats a host like that?"

"I'm not your guest!" you shout.

Strahd gives you a weary and disappointed shrug. Then he punches you in the chest.

You fly backward as if you'd been kicked by an angry

horse. The impact sends you reeling into one of the posts on the bed behind you, and it snaps in half, the black canopy spilling down over you.

Desperate to untangle yourself, you claw back the fabric and see that Strahd is already standing over you, scowling into your face. "This is precisely the sort of thing I was hoping to avoid," he says, and he clucks his tongue at the broken bedpost. "Do you know how hard it is to find a good joiner in Barovia?"

Your hand trembles in fear as you raise your holy symbol once more, but Strahd backhands it away. It flies from your grasp and goes clattering across the floor.

"Don't be an idiot," he says with a vicious snarl. "If such trinkets bothered me, don't you think I would have had it removed while you slept?"

Strahd grabs you by the throat and lifts you to your feet. His fangs are longer now than before: sharp, wet, and ready.

"I could kill you right now," he says.

You try to pry his fingers away from your neck, but they hold you as fast as an iron collar. You don't doubt that he's right, that he could murder you in an instant.

"If you wanted to do that, I'd already be dead," you manage to choke out.

He admits your correctness with a grim nod and releases your neck. Your legs lacking all strength, you collapse to the carpet beneath you. As you gasp for breath, you see a set of booted feet walk into the room and halt behind

Strahd's cape, and you discover that the two of you are no longer alone.

The vampire lord steps aside to reveal a pale-skinned soldier who stares at you with wide, hungry eyes.

"I no longer have any use for you," Strahd says as you push yourself to your feet. "But the same isn't true for my friend here. Since you have proven yourself to be the worst sort of guest, I'll leave you to his tender mercies."

With that, the vampire lord dissolves into a cloud of mist that disappears beneath the door the soldier closed behind himself. Alone with the soldier, you look into his eyes as he bares his savage fangs, and you realize that you've already made your final mistake.

THE END

Defenseless as you are, you realize you're no match for a pack of hungry wolves. They prowl around you, fanning out, trying to surround you on all sides. If they manage to encircle you, they're sure to attack.

You utter a quick prayer to Tyr and touch the holy symbol hanging around your neck. It bursts into a brilliant light, and you hold it out before you.

Startled by your supernatural feat, the wolves—who'd been growing closer—back away with a chorus of whimpers. Still, they don't take their eyes off you. They lick their chops as they look to find a way past your light.

You know that it's only a matter of time until one of the wolves decides to test you. When it does, the pack will discover that the light is just that: a light. It might be blinding in the darkness, but it doesn't burn and cannot harm.

And when they realize they have nothing to fear, they'll take you down. Before that happens, you need to take advantage of their momentary fear and flee.

Keeping your blazing holy symbol before you, you turn toward the front gates of Castle Ravenloft, and you run.

Turn to page 15 . . .

You utter a short prayer to Tyr and point at the end of the werewolf's snout. It bursts into a bright light that blinds the creature. The beast howls in protest, but you ignore that and smack it in the face with your glowing hammer.

The werewolf tumbles over backward, one of its fangs flying loose. The other wolves stare at it in stunned silence.

You raise the hammer to strike again, but the werewolf leaps to its feet before you can land another blow.

"Was gonna let you live," the werewolf growls through a snout never meant for human speech. "No more!"

The werewolf stalks toward you, and you back away, confident it can't see you. It pricks up its ears as you move, though, and its nostrils flare as it sniffs the air.

"Think you can get away that easy?" The werewolf chuckles. "I hunt in the dark. The last thing I need is my eyes."

You swing at the creature with your hammer, and it connects with its shoulder. It ignores the pain, though, and claws its way inside the hammer's reach to grab you by your shirt.

The fabric tears as you pull away and scream in protest, but the werewolf just laughs as its teeth cut your cries short.

THE END

You're not about to go down without a fight. You spit out a quick desperate prayer and hold out your hands before you in fists. A glowing hammer made of transparent mystical energies appears before you, floating in midair.

One of the wolves leaps at you, its slavering jaws wide. With a gesture, you bring the glowing hammer around and smack the wolf across the side of its head. It scrambles backward, whimpering in pain.

You allow yourself a smile as the rest of the wolves back up, cautious now at this display of your power. But one of the wolves refuses to retreat.

Instead, as you watch, it hoists itself up and balances on its hind legs. Then it lets out an earsplitting howl as it begins to grow thicker and stronger, forming the shape of a furry man with savage claws and a massive wolf's head.

The beast was hiding among the wolves, but it isn't any mere wolf. You see the creature now for what it is: half human, half beast. A snarling, savage werewolf!

You bring your glowing hammer between you and the beast. It flexes its arms and then lets loose another dreadful howl at the full moon.

Fight! Turn to page 4 . . .
Blind it with a light spell to the face! Turn to page 13 . . .

You're halfway to the castle's exit when you see through the mist that the arch that leads out through the thick stone wall is sealed by the iron bars of a portcullis. "Help!" you shout, hoping that there might be someone in the guardhouse to save you.

You offer up another prayer to Tyr, but he seems to be too busy to lend you any direct aid.

A wolf nips at your heels, its teeth gnashing the air right behind you. Summoning your mystic powers, you point and bark an order at it. "Flee!"

The wolf skids to a halt, then turns and sprints away from you as fast as it can. Unfortunately, you don't have enough power to handle all the beasts that way. The rest of the wolves stare after their friend for a moment, confused, but this buys you only an instant of respite.

You reach the portcullis and try to squirm your way between its wrought-iron bars, but you're not slender enough. A wolf's jaws close on one of your forearms, and the beast begins hauling you back.

Maybe you could have prevailed against the one wolf, but there are so many of them—far too many. Soon, they fill the moonlit sky with howls of triumph.

THE END

As the count leaves the room, you let the door close behind him. You return to the bed and sit on the edge of it for a moment as you contemplate the choices you've made in your life that have somehow led you to this moment.

Did you offend Tyr in some way? Did he mean for the vampire to capture you as punishment for something you did wrong? Or is this, perhaps, a test of your faith? Of your steadfastness? Of your ability to help yourself?

Or maybe this has nothing to do with Tyr. Maybe the vampire just saw you and picked you out at random, an unfortunate victim on whom to visit his horrible plans, whatever they might be.

Falling to your knees, you pray to Tyr for guidance, but he doesn't answer. Then again, it's rare for gods to communicate directly with their followers, even so devout a priest as you. The need for justice speaks for itself, and you have your studies of Tyr's word to guide you.

Still, the time spent in prayer helps to clear your head and strengthen your resolve to find a way out. After rising to your feet, you search the room. If Strahd still has your armor and weapons, he didn't leave them here. There's a large walk-in closet, but there's nothing in it but a dusty black cloak hanging from a hook in the far wall.

Donning the cloak, you return to the bedroom. Seeing no other escape, you sidle up to the door and listen at it, wondering if Strahd is on the opposite side, waiting for you to emerge. After a long moment, you decide to chance it and crack open the door.

It creaks on its ancient hinges with a noise so loud you wonder if it could alert the entire castle. There's a room beyond, although you can't see much of it through the crack. Shoving the door entirely open, you wait in the doorway, breathless, looking for any sign of Strahd or his underlings.

Not even a mouse comes to investigate.

You breathe again and step over the threshold. Thunder shakes the tower from some distant storm that doesn't seem to have broken yet, at least not that you can see through the wide windows of leaded glass that occupy the opposite wall. Three ornate lanterns hang from the ceiling in this room, and by their dim glow, you can see a pair of overstuffed couches and a bulging bookshelf.

You examine the books, hoping they might provide some clue for escaping your predicament, but the titles prove useless in that regard. They include *Embalming: The Lost Art, Life Among the Undead: Learning to Cope, Castle Building 101,* and *Goats of the Balinok Mountains*. Several of them seem to have been written by Strahd himself.

Looking around, you spy another door on the far end of the bookshelf and pad over to it as silently as you can manage. It creaks when you open it, but not nearly as loudly as the door to the bedchamber did. Beyond, you find a smaller room shrouded in darkness.

There are no loose lanterns around, only ones attached to bolts or chains, so you go back to the bedroom in which you woke and break one of the posts from the bed. You wind strips of the bedsheets around the end of it, and then you light your makeshift torch, using the flames from one of the lanterns bolted to the wall near the bookshelf. Now you're ready to deal with whatever the darkness holds for you—or so you hope.

You return to the darkened room and discover that a portrait of Strahd hangs on the wall to your left. A spiral stairway just beyond the portrait leads upward, and another spiral stairway next to it leads downward.

You bring your torch closer and see that this image shows Strahd from the days before his transformation. His eyes seem to follow you no matter where you move.

The portrait disturbs you so much that you back away onto the carpet on the far side of the room. As you step upon it, the rug curls up at its edges and attacks. Rising, it tries to wrap itself around you, but you leap away before its gets your entire body in its grip, leaving it clinging to only your legs.

You slam your torch down onto the rug, and it recoils as you singe its threads. Pressing your advantage, you shove the torch into it over and over until the entire thing catches fire.

The rug goes up fast, and you find yourself grateful that the tower's floor here is made of stone. You look at the portrait of Strahd and find it glaring at you.

"Leave me alone," you tell it, "and you won't share the rug's fate."

It's time to move on.

Descend the stairs. Turn to page 26 . . .

Ascend the stairs. Turn to page 28 . . .

Using your holy symbol to display your faith might not affect a creature as powerful as Strahd, but Tyr's favor has often proven strong enough for you to drive lesser undead away. "Get back," you say as the strange thing lowers itself next to you. "The power of Tyr protects me."

The creature offers you a tinny laugh. You can see it clearly now, and you realize that it's neither living nor undead but a construct, a clockwork creature built to resemble a small man in the clothes of a court jester. His skin is made of leather strapped over an iron framework, and you can hear his motors clicking and clacking as he moves.

"You don't need that with me," the creature says. His jaw flaps as he speaks, but otherwise his face doesn't move. You can't tell if he's friendly or murderous.

"Don't I? How can I know that?" you ask.

The creature's jaw drops. "You can hear me? No one ever hears me."

Sensing the grace of Tyr's favor upon you, you offer up a prayer of thanks to your chosen god. "That must mean we're meant to be friends. What's your name?"

The creature fidgets before answering, still confused by your apparent luck. "Pidlwick. I'm looking for my friend," Pidlwick says as he turns his head all around. "Will you help me find him?"

Ask for Pidlwick's help instead. Turn to page 31...

Tell Pidlwick to go away. Turn to page 33...

Help Pidlwick find his friend. Turn to page 36...

"I just want to stretch my legs for a little bit first," you tell Cyrus. You hope to buy some time before the oddly made person calls Strahd for help. Was he born that way, you wonder, or did Strahd somehow transform him? In the end, you suppose it doesn't make much of a difference.

The only important thing is that he serves Strahd and isn't going to help you to escape. You think you could take Cyrus down if you needed to, but it seems a shame to harm such a wretched creature—unless he forces your hand. Tyr calls you to work toward justice, after all.

"The master is very strict about how his guests are permitted to behave," Cyrus says, squirming with agitation. "If he finds you down here, he won't like it. He won't like it at all."

"Since he kidnapped me, I don't much care what he likes or doesn't like," you say. "In fact, making him angry would only make me happy."

Cyrus's face twists with dismay. He begins to slap himself on the head over and over, wincing in pain each time. "The master. Will. Not. Be. Pleased!"

Then he begins to weep openly, although you cannot tell if it's from the pain of his blows or just because he's upset. Either way, you're not about to try to comfort someone who wants nothing more than to turn you back over to Strahd. Instead, you ignore him and poke around the hall.

There's a wide set of doors to the left, three different doors in the wall ahead—along with a set of stairs leading upward—and a rusty portcullis to the right. Through the bars of the portcullis, you can see stacks of wine casks, and you wonder if the wine has gone sour after so many years sitting there untouched.

"Knock-knock," Cyrus says.

You're not even sure if he's talking to you, but you decide to play along. "Who's there?" you respond.

The man flinches as if you've brandished a sword at him. Then he peers into the darkness, toward something you couldn't possibly see, and whispers, "Master?"

Then he starts giggling madly, and you wonder just who the joke might be on.

You shake your head at him and head for the doors to the left. They're banded in steel, but they look more promising than trying your luck with the rusty bars.

"No," Cyrus says, shaking his head. "Don't go in there. Too dangerous. Far too dangerous." He sidles toward the door through which you entered and beckons for you to follow.

"Come with me," he says.

Can you trust him? you wonder. "I don't want to see your master."

Cyrus giggles. "No, no, no!"

He's so pathetic. But maybe he's right. . . .

Follow Cyrus. Turn to page 81 . . .
Ignore Cyrus. Turn to page 41 . . .

You can't just let something as amazing as a gigantic crystal the size of a horse-drawn carriage hang here in Castle Ravenloft without checking it out. You start climbing the stairs in hope of getting close enough to get a better look at it—or maybe even destroy it.

As you climb higher, the tower trembles harder and harder with every beat of the great red crystal. Without any railing on the stairwell, you have to cling to the wall to keep yourself from being thrown into the tower's central well and falling to your death. Fortunately, the crystal pulses to a regular rhythm, so you can predict just when each tremor is about to start.

You keep climbing the stairs, moving as fast as you can safely manage. The light from the crystal, which was fairly faint when viewed from the bottom of the tower, soon suffuses everything. It seems as though all it touches is covered in blood.

By the time you reach the crystal's level, the floor of the tower has disappeared into blackness below you. You have no doubt what your fate would be if you fell.

Turn to page 55...

You don't see how going upward would help you to leave the castle, so you take the spiral staircase downward instead. As you go, you come across a number of different landings, but you ignore them and keep going down, down, down.

Eventually, you reach the bottom of the stairs and see that they emerge into a long hallway filled with still black water as far as you can see by the flickering light of your torch. You decide that this doesn't look inviting. It's one thing to be trapped in Castle Ravenloft, but you'd rather not add "soaking wet" to your list of miseries.

You head back up the stairs to the next landing above instead. There you find an oaken door and push it open. It leads into a large hallway filled to your waist with fog. As you move out into it, you turn to your right and see a dark figure holding a lantern high over its head. It has its back to you, and you hold your breath, hoping to avoid detection.

The figure cocks its head as if it hears you and then spins about and begins moving in your direction. As it nears with a shuffling gait, you can make out a warped person with fur on one side of his face and scales on the other. He has a hunched back, and small tusks jut from his lower jaw. The ears of a large cat sit atop his head, and you can hear one of his feet flapping with every step as he nears you.

"Oh," he says in a dismayed tone. "You're one of the master's guests, aren't you? You shouldn't be roaming about the castle like this. It's not permitted, you know."

"Who are you?" you ask, hoping to change the subject.

"Why, I'm Cyrus." He wheezes with a little cough. "Cyrus Belview. Count Strahd's faithful servant. I live to make the master happy. Or at least not quite as angry as he usually is."

He gives you a sidelong look. "You really ought to return to your chamber. I'd be honored to lead you back there if you're lost."

Turn to page 22 . . .

You decide that down seems dangerous and that it's smarter to head upward, where you can get a better look at wherever—and whatever—Castle Ravenloft is. At the top of the stairs, you reach the roof of the tower. You walk to the crenellations lining the edge of the circular roof and gaze out over what you can see of the castle under the muted moonlight of the cloudy sky.

Castle Ravenloft is a stunning yet creepy feast for the eyes. Towers spike from its main building in several different places. Once upon a time, it must have been an amazing palace. Now it's become a decrepit and haunted wreck.

Off to the north, there's a bridge that connects the tower you're on to a taller tower on the north side of the castle. You could cross it, but there's no railing. Falling off the side would mean tumbling into the courtyard, which yawns nearly two hundred feet below.

The tower that you're on top of sits near the center of the castle. It also butts up against the outside of yet another tower that stretches skyward next to it. The other tower has no windows or doors that you can see. Unless you can figure out how to walk through walls, there's no way into it.

As you contemplate praying to Tyr for a spell that could deliver you safely to the ground from your perch high above Ravenloft's courtyard, you lean against the other tower. You look above you, and you see a spindly little man hanging in the vines that spiral along the tower.

The man—if that's in fact what he is—looks down at you with unblinking eyes that glitter in the moonlight.

He doesn't say a word. He just hangs there like a spider in a web.

"Hello," you call softly. You're not sure this is wise. The man could easily call out to Strahd and expose your attempt to escape from the castle. The fact that he hasn't done so yet gives you a sliver of hope that you might have somehow found an ally.

The man doesn't respond. Instead, he creeps closer, climbing down the vines headfirst, never taking his eyes off you. As he nears, you realize that he isn't human at all. He's about the size of a halfling or gnome, but he doesn't belong to either race.

Whatever he is, he's not breathing. Could he be an undead creature encased in some sort of elaborate armor? You wouldn't put it beyond Strahd to be so cunning.

You put a hand on your holy symbol and then raise it before you to ward off the undead. You're not sure if it'll work against this creature, but you don't have many other options at hand.

Turn to page 21 . . .

With the torch by your side, you strum the harp's strings and find it surprisingly well-tuned. You sit to play a hymn to Tyr, if only to calm Pidlwick for a moment. As you do, a ghostly figure appears next to you, nodding along with your tune. The ghost is dressed like Pidlwick and stands exactly as tall.

When the ghost doesn't attack, you keep playing. As you finish, the ghost asks, "Why have you summoned me from beyond the grave?"

You point at Pidlwick, and the clockwork creature gives the ghost a tenuous wave.

The ghost scowls. "You? How dare you darken my domain! If it wasn't for you, I'd still be alive." The ghost turns to you. "This creature replaced me!"

"That hardly cost you your life," you point out to the ghostly figure.

"No!" the ghost splutters. "That happened when he led me up into the high tower and pushed me down the stairs!"

The ghost turns on his clockwork substitute. "I thought I told you what would happen to you the last time you came here to taunt me. Prepare to meet your end!"

Stop the ghost. Turn to page 50 . . .
Help the ghost. Turn to page 54 . . .

I'm sorry," you say. "But I need to get out of here and fast. If you help me, then I'll pray to Tyr to assist in your reunion with your friend."

Pidlwick considers your offer.

"I guess I can always go looking for my friend later," he says finally, with a hint of resentment.

Despite any hard feelings, he dutifully leads you down the stairwell by which you reached this rooftop. With a mixture of hope and mistrust, you follow him.

You hold your torch up before you, illuminating the way, although the clockwork jester doesn't seem to need it. The two of you pass several landings, and at each one you wonder if the creature will stop. Instead, he keeps waddling down, down, down.

Eventually, you reach the bottom. There's no place lower left to go. The stairwell emerges into a long, wide hallway that's covered with black water so smooth and still it's like a mirror. Pidlwick doesn't hesitate before plunging in.

For a moment, you fear that the creature might be lost under the water, leaving nothing but ripples to mark his passing. Fortunately, the water proves to be only a few feet deep, leaving Pidlwick's head exposed.

You hesitate at the water's edge, unsure that you want to enter. Who knows what its surface might conceal?

The clockwork jester realizes that you've stopped, and he turns around to gaze back at you.

Turn to page 34 . . .

The last thing you need is one of Strahd's minions pretending to help you, ready to sell you out and scream for help the next chance he gets. You decide you can't trust the creature any further than you could throw him.

"I think I'll be fine on my own," you say to Pidlwick.

The creature fidgets and lowers his eyes, looking as disappointed as an animated doll can manage. "It's a dangerous place," Pidlwick says. "Very dangerous."

You edge away from the thing, moving toward the bridge to the other tower. "Good luck finding your friend," you say in what you hope the creature can understand as a goodbye tone.

As you move onto the bridge, you see a glow emanating from the doorway that leads into the opposite tower. This intrigues you, drawing you closer. You're so enthralled by it that you don't hear the *tik-tik-tik* of Pidlwick's footsteps coming up behind you until it's far too late.

"Very dangerous!" the little creature shouts as he plows into you, shoving you to the side. You windmill your arms, looking for purchase, hoping to regain your balance. Instead, you topple into the open air and fall to your doom far below.

THE END

"Come on now," Pidlwick says as he beckons you into the water. "There's nothing to be afraid of here. If it won't dissolve me, it won't dissolve you, right?"

You hesitate. "Isn't there a better way? Perhaps we could go back upstairs a few levels."

The jester shrugs, and the bells on his hat jingle. "It's far more dangerous up there. Believe me, I've been all over the castle, and the upper levels are the worst parts. Down here is the safest."

"But I don't want to be safe," you point out. "I want to leave."

"Right!" Pidlwick says with a little leap as if you just reminded him of something. Then he stops and looks wistfully off into the distance. "You know, I've never been outside the castle walls."

A wave of pity ripples through you. "Maybe you could come with me."

Pidlwick giggles. "I'd like that. I think."

He jerks his head toward the inky waters. "So, what's it going to be? Am I going to lead or are you?"

Let Pidlwick lead. Turn to page 38 . . .
Take the lead yourself. Turn to page 65 . . .

As you walk up to the stained-glass window, you see that it's too dirty for any light to pass through. While you peer closer, footsteps stampede up behind you.

Pidlwick charges straight at you, hoping to push you through the window, but you turn just in time to swing gracefully out of his way, and he zips past you, smashing through the dazzling stained glass. He sails right over the knee-high windowsill and plunges into the darkness beyond.

You edge up to the hole and peer through the broken window. From here, it's a sharp drop down the face of a cliff, but you think you can see the valley floor nearly a thousand feet below. While it's sure to be a hard climb, it shouldn't be impossible.

Steeling yourself, you offer up what you hope won't be your final prayer to Tyr and begin making your way down the side of the cliff. What seems like hours later, you find yourself on safer, flatter ground, and free of Castle Ravenloft.

THE END

Pidlwick claps his metallic hands with glee. "Really?" he cries. "Thank you so much! I can't wait for you to meet my friend."

The little creature waddles over to the stairwell that you climbed up to get to the roof and beckons for you to follow him. You do so but from a distance, concerned that the *tik-tik-tik* of Pidlwick's walk might draw unwelcome attention.

He leads you all the way past the landing where you entered the stairwell and down to the next floor. "Careful here." He points at shadowy alcoves set to either side of an intricately engraved steel door before you that seems to shine with a light of its own. A figure stands obscured in each of those niches.

The two figures begin to squirm in inhuman ways. Pidlwick cackles and dances about in some sort of crazed delight. Cautious, you push your torch ahead of you, and each of the figures dissolves into a swarm of black-furred rats that dash straight for you.

You flail about, swinging your torch left and right. One blow smacks a particularly large rat in the head, and it bursts into flames. The fire catches quickly among the others—with a bit of help from more such blows—and soon the surviving rats flee for less-lethal locations.

"Thank you!" Pidlwick cries as he comes up and hugs your legs. "I haven't been able to get past those nasty creatures for years."

You pull yourself out of the little thing's grasp and motion for him to open the door. He prances over to it and hauls it open on well-oiled hinges. Without any further ceremony, he charges into the chamber beyond, a formal dining room in which every item of furniture is covered with a thick layer of dust.

A disused harp stands in one corner of the room, and Pidlwick points at it and shouts, "Play it! Play it!"

Turn to page 30 . . .

You defer to Pidlwick with a graceful bow. The creature leaps in joy so much that he makes waves in the water.

"Thank you, thank you, thank you!" he cries. "This'll make everything so much easier."

"How do you mean?" you ask as you dip your toes in the water for the first time. It feels cold and smells stale, with an underlying scent of rot. The whole idea repulses you, but if the only way out of Castle Ravenloft is in this direction, you're determined to put up with it.

The water reaches to your waist as you move farther in, making you cringe from more than just the chill. You swear that you can feel things moving in the fluid, as if you're wading through some sort of disgusting soup made of bones and long-dissolved flesh, and you have to stop for a moment to stifle the urge to retch.

As disgusting as it all is, Pidlwick doesn't seem affected in the slightest. Only his head remains visible above the water's surface, but it zips back and forth as the little creature zooms down the darkened passageway. Unwilling to be left behind, you hold your torch high over your head to keep it dry and to help illuminate your way.

You follow Pidlwick as best you can, moving straight behind him no matter how much he diverts left and right. He starts humming a morose tune that you don't recognize, probably something popular long before you were born.

As you move along the hallway, the ground beneath your feet suddenly gives way. Surprised, you fall through a trapdoor hidden under the water and plunge into a flooded pit below. As you hit the bottom, there's a bright flash and you suddenly find yourself elsewhere.

Turn to page 44 . . .

You know where Cyrus's loyalties lie, and you're not about to let him lead you back to Strahd's so-called hospitality. If he's afraid to go through those doors at the end of the hall, that's exactly what you're going to do. At least then, you hope, he won't follow you.

The doors are heavy, but they're not locked. You pull on the one to the right, and it swings toward you on creaky hinges. Cyrus lets out a little squeal of terror at the noise, flings up his arms, and then scutters away.

As you walk through the door, a sense of foreboding evil permeates the room, making you want to gag. It stinks of the rot of death and the coppery tang of old blood.

The floor is covered with dark stains that you'd rather not think about. The remnants of several oaken tables and chairs lie scattered about in splintered pieces. Most of the wood has been shoved up against the walls to make room for a newer set of furniture constructed entirely from human bones. This includes a long dining table surrounded by ten high-backed chairs.

The walls and ceiling—which vaults twenty feet high—have been decorated with bones as well, attached in intricate patterns that you find disturbing to look at. Worse, though, are the four piles of skulls, one in each corner of the room. Garlands of skulls reach from each of those stacks to a chandelier fashioned from bones that hangs in the center of the room, right over the dining table.

There are doors that lead out of the room at either end. Both of these are sheathed in bones. The doors you

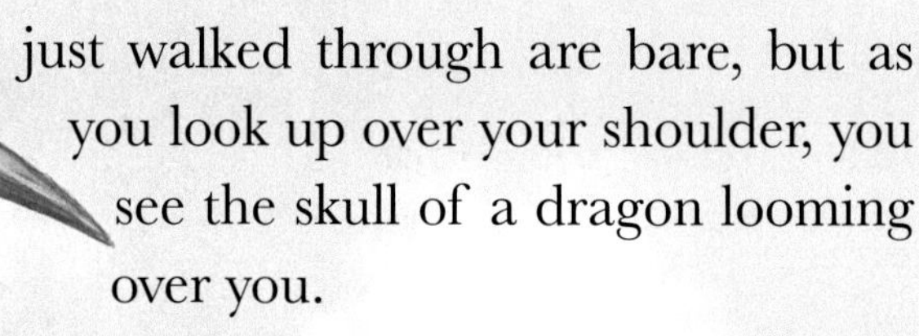

just walked through are bare, but as you look up over your shoulder, you see the skull of a dragon looming over you.

You start to think that maybe Cyrus had a point.

Not wanting to be crushed, you move out from under the dragon's skull. Leaving the room quickly seems like an excellent idea, so you pick a door fast and head through the one on the left. This leads you to a smaller room that shows signs of a struggle that happened long ago. A handful of skeletons are scattered about the place, laying amid shattered furniture and dented armor. At least no one's gone to the trouble to redecorate the place as they did the dining room.

An open passageway leads to the right, and you follow it past a set of alcoves that must have once served as quarters, perhaps for the people who were killed in the last room. There's a staircase at the far end, leading up. You climb it, hoping to find a lot less death at the top.

You emerge in a wide circular chamber with a passageway that leads left. There's an open spiral staircase that leads upward—bereft of any railing—hugging the curves of the room's wall. This must be the base of the castle's north tower.

When you left the bedchamber, you'd planned to find your way to the main floor and then look for a way to leave, but when you gaze up, the most amazing sight beckons you higher. A couple of hundred feet above you, a gigantic blood-red crystal hangs suspended in the tower's heights. It glows with a crimson light and pulsates with the rhythm of a heart, as if it's the organ that pumps power throughout the entire complex.

As the heart pulses, the entire tower shudders with every beat. You stare up at it in awe, wondering what kind of crazed magic it represents. Clearly, it must be important to Strahd, and that makes you feel like you might want to destroy it, if only to stop him from kidnapping anyone else—and otherwise terrorizing the people of Barovia—ever again.

You're just not sure that doing so is more important than escaping with your life.

Investigate the giant crystal. Turn to page 25 . . .
Look for a way out. Turn to page 49 . . .

You've been teleported somewhere! For an instant, you hope you've been brought to someplace safe and dry, but that's dashed as you find yourself immersed in dark water. Your torch has gone out, of course, so you can't see a thing, but when you put your feet down, you strike solid ground.

When you stand up, you find you can raise your head out of the water, but you're submerged from the neck down. As you feel around in the darkness, you discover that you're in a prison cell and that the lock set in the solid iron bars has long since rusted stuck.

You hear Pidlwick singing in the distance, his voice echoing off unseen walls.

"Help!" you call out. "Pidlwick! Help!" But he only cackles with glee and then falls silent. You scream, you beg, you plead for someone, anyone, to come and help you, but no one responds.

Frightened and cold as you are, you try to stay awake as long as you can—for what seems like days—but eventually you're too tired to stand any longer. As your legs give out, you slip beneath the water's surface, and it ripples around you no more.

THE END

"I can't have you dragging me around to every corner of this castle of the damned, looking for people to save," you inform Escher. "I need to leave here right away. Maybe once I'm free I can find some help and come back to save this Gertruda."

Escher shakes his head, terribly amused. "Firstly, Gertruda is sure to have been taken by Strahd long before you could return. Secondly, the idea that you could lead an assault on Castle Ravenloft and destroy its master? Let's just say that many others have tried."

You put your hands on your hips. "None of them were me."

Escher throws his hands in the air in mock surrender and laughs. "Fair enough. In that case, I retract my offer. Clearly, I need to worry more about you than Gertruda."

As you narrow your eyes at him, you put your hand on your holy symbol and begin to look for escape routes. "Just what do you mean by that?"

"I don't need you to rid me of Gertruda. I'd be perfectly happy just to have you rid Castle Ravenloft of yourself — and I'm willing to help make that happen. Peacefully, I hope."

Maybe you can relax just a hair. "So you'll show me the way out? No strings attached?"

"None." He turns on his heel and begins walking away. "Just be sure to keep up. We need to be fast. If Strahd sees us, you can be sure I won't be the one who's doomed."

Escher leads you back into the main part of the castle through the archway where you exited the tower. He goes back into the tower, walks quickly along the landing on that level, and ducks into a darkened hallway you'd ignored in favor of the open air.

Alcoves line both sides of the hallway, each filled with a life-size and lifelike statue. As a bolt of lightning flashes outside, you swear that the faces of the statues transform from serene and proud to screaming and disappointed, but that fades faster than the thunder that shakes the castle.

"Strahd's ancestors," Escher says with a dismissive wave. "Forever anguished about how their bloodline turned out, I'd think."

At the end of the hallway, Escher turns down a narrow stairway that eventually leads you to a blank wall decorated with oak paneling. He pushes on the frame of one of the panels, and a hidden door swings outward to reveal yet another hallway.

A pair of double doors is set on each side. Escher chooses the set on the right, and you follow him into a throne room. An ornate chair sits at the far end, clearly meant for the ruler when he received people at court.

"Note how the throne faces away from the rest of the room?" Escher says. "Says a lot, don't you think?"

Before you can answer, Escher turns from the throne and strides toward a set of stairs. These descend to a large landing that leads to a stairwell wide enough to drive a dragon through.

Following this brings you to a massive entry hall, which features a domed ceiling held up by four large pillars.

Gargoyles grin down at you from the dome's rim, but despite your worries, they don't move.

Escher strides off to the right and flings open a large pair of doors. As he does, he skids to a stop and puts his hands on his hips.

You come up behind Escher and see a dark-haired elf decked out in fine clothing blocking his path.

"Rahadin," Escher says to the elf with a firm nod. "What is the count's chamberlain doing skulking about at this hour?"

The elf peers around Escher at you, a vicious snarl on his lips. "Apparently keeping you from betraying Count Strahd's interests."

Escher brings you forward. "Well, that's just not true," he says. "Is it?" he asks you.

Turn Escher in. Turn to page 90 . . .

Lie for Escher. Turn to page 89 . . .

You take the passageway to the left and find yourself at the base of the turret, just left of the main doors. This would be wonderful if you were skinny enough to slip through one of the tall narrow windows, but they're barely wide enough for an archer to fire an arrow through, let alone for you to squeeze through.

Heading back the way you came, you return to the original tower. You'd rather not go downward to chat with Cyrus once more, so instead you make your way up the massive staircase, bringing you closer to the giant crystal floating above. On reaching the first landing, you explore further but have no more luck, so you head back to the tower with the crystal and climb to the next landing. There, you discover an archway that leads outside.

A ten-foot-wide walkway winds around the front of the castle, jutting out from the main part of the castle to the top of the outer wall that surrounds and protects the entire place. You creep along it, hoping that no one spots you.

Turn to page 60 . . .

You snatch up your holy symbol and flash it in front of the ghost. "By the power of Tyr, I demand you leave this creature be!"

The ghost sneers at you. "Your god holds no sway over me," he says. He grabs the clockwork creature by the arm, and the leather skin holding the arm together withers away to dust. The creature squeals in terror and dismay.

Appalled, you pick up your torch and swing it at the ghost, but it passes right through him, leaving only a chill running up your arm and down your spine. It does get the ghost to drop the clockwork creature, though. Unfortunately, the ghost turns his attention to you instead.

The ghost glowers at you, and his lively yet transparent face transforms into a horrifying vision of death, rotten from the passing of the years. You scream in terror as he reaches for you, and curl up into a ball at his feet.

As you lie there on the ground, the ghost punches at you with his fists. Each time they pass through you, you feel your skin, muscles, and even bones wither and rot away. It's not long before you wheeze your last breath.

THE END

The ghost keeps swiping away at the fake jester until every bit of the leather holding him together rots to dust.

"Please, finish him off," the ghost says. "I can't do it."

Cautiously, you take your foot off the remnants of the clockwork creature. "You seem to have done a fine job so far."

The ghost gives you an enthusiastic nod. "Yes, I've disabled him, but I can't physically touch him to destroy him, just age the parts that can be aged. If someone who knew what they were doing got ahold of him, they might be able to piece him back together. He's like a puppet that's had its strings snipped."

You nod, understanding. "And we can't leave him for someone to restring."

"Exactly."

Staring down at the seemingly lifeless puppet, you see that there's still a glint in his artificial eyes. "And you don't think this is punishment enough?"

"Would you like to be stuck here, staring at the ceiling of this room for eternity? You'd be doing him a favor."

With a frown as you steel yourself for the distasteful task, you raise your foot and start stomping. You don't stop until the light fades from the unholy creature's eyes.

"That's wonderful work there," the ghost says to you with no little pride. "We make an excellent team."

You don't smile. Destroying things—even if they are evil things—is grim work.

"I don't suppose I've impressed you enough that you could show me the way out of here?" you ask the ghost.

The ghost shrugs. "I honestly wish I could, but there's just no way."

You narrow your eyes at him. "What do you mean? It's hopeless?"

The ghost rises into the air and hovers over the dining table in the middle of the room. You notice there's a tall cake of many layers sitting in the middle of it. It's so old that the frosting has turned from white to a sickly green. There's a figurine of a woman in a wedding dress standing on top of it.

"You see this cake?" the ghost says. "This was baked for the wedding of Tatyana – the woman Strahd loved – to his younger brother, Sergei. He murdered them on their wedding night."

"God!"

The ghost shakes his head. "That was four hundred years ago. No one has dined in this room since."

"Then how did you end up here?"

"I died here." The ghost points to the room's entrance. "I crawled in here after that monstrosity pushed me down the stairs, and I breathed my last in this room. And so I'm bound here, trapped forever."

"How horrible!" you say. "To be alone for so long. How can you bear it?"

"It's been hard," the ghost says. "Some days, I think perhaps I've gone mad."

He shoots you a look that makes you uncomfortable. There are two other doorways out of the room, beside the one you came in through, and there is a set of windows that overlook the courtyard, some ninety feet below. Your best bet is perhaps to go back the way you came.

"You know what would really help with my loneliness?" the ghost asks you.

"No," you say, fairly sure that you don't want to know the answer.

"Company!"

The ghost dives at you, making your entire body go numb. Then your limbs start moving about on their own, and you realize you're no longer in control. You start back up the steps, and a moment later you come tumbling down, hard and fast.

Sometime later you wake to find that your body has disappeared, but you still remain—as a brand-new ghost.

THE END

Given the situation, you don't owe your creepy little guide anything, and the ghost is perfectly justified in being angry with him. In fact, you're pretty sure the clockwork jester brought you down here in an effort to trick the ghost into killing you.

You're going to make sure the creature gets what he deserves.

The ghost slashes at the creature's arm, and where his fingers pass through the leather skin, it rots to nothing.

The clockwork jester squeals in dismay and looks to you for help. "Please, friend!" he says.

"You're no friend of mine," you tell him as you kick the creature over onto his back. He tries to squirm away from the ghost's attacks, but you stand on his useless arm, pinning it to the ground.

"But you're a cleric!" the creature says as he tries to push you off. "A good cleric!"

The ghost swipes at the creature's other arm, and the leather bits holding it together turn to dust.

"I'm a cleric of Tyr, god of justice," you inform the creature. "And justice is exactly what murderers like you deserve. Prepare to meet oblivion!"

Turn to page 51 . . .

You've been so transfixed by the giant crystal heart pounding at the top of the tower that you entirely missed another odd fact about the place. There's not a single window in the whole height of it. Perhaps that's why you're so surprised when Strahd strolls down from where the stairwell leads past the heart, as if he's been waiting on the roof above it the entire time.

"So," he says with a cold smile, "you've decided to spurn my hospitality. We take such insults very seriously here in Barovia."

You scowl at his false offense. "If I had a spear, I'd hurl it straight through your heart!"

He chuckles at your bravado. "Do you mean the one in my chest or the Heart of Sorrow?" He gestures at the giant crystal. "Either way, I'm afraid you've overstayed your welcome. The penalty for that is rather permanent."

With that, he chants a few magic words and gestures in your direction. A tremendous gust of wind springs out of nowhere and lifts you from your feet. As you realize his intention, you reach for something to grab hold of, but it's too late.

You scream all the way down.

THE END

"Thanks for the offer to help me escape," you tell Pidlwick, "but I can handle it from here."

Pidlwick clucks his mechanical tongue at you. "If you ignore my advice, you're asking for trouble." He shudders. "Around here, trouble means death."

At this point you're willing to risk it. You open the door on the left—the "dangerous" one—and discover a long, straight stairway leading upward. Despite Pidlwick's protests, you begin climbing the steps, as carefully and quietly as you can manage.

About halfway up, the stairs curve to the right. You rest on the landing for a moment and then continue. When you reach the top, you find a large wooden door. As you push it open gently, its hinges creak loudly enough to wake the dead.

The room beyond is a well-kept office. There's a large table inside, with a tall chair behind it. Stacks of papers sit neatly organized on the table, next to an inkwell and a quill in a stand.

The oak-paneled walls feature lances, swords, and shields of all sorts, each emblazoned with a seal that you realize must belong to either Strahd or Barovia. You're not sure if there's any distinction between the two.

No windows appear here—the only light comes from your torch—which makes you think you might still be underground. You turn, about to ask Pidlwick about the place, but the clockwork jester slips back into the stairwell and slams the door in your face.

From this side, the door disappears into the oak paneling. You reach for it, but there's no obvious handle.

As you search for purchase on the door, someone clears his throat behind you. You whirl around and find a black-haired elf with violet skin staring at you. He blocks the room's only apparent exit.

"Greetings. I assume you're the latest of Count Strahd's guests."

As the elf speaks, the screaming of multiple men and women works its way into your head. Sensing the horror that now fills your brain, the elf smirks at you. You try to shake your head to dislodge the sound. It quietens but doesn't disappear completely.

"It seems so," you say, bringing your torch between you and the elf, who casts a strange shadow on the wall behind him. He seems to be breathing—unlike most of the creatures here—but that doesn't make him any less dangerous. "And who might you be?"

The elf puts a hand to his chest and gives you a little bow. "My name is Rahadin, and I'm the count's chamberlain. I'm in charge of the day-to-day operations of Castle Ravenloft. There's little that transpires here of which I'm not aware."

"So you knew he'd be kidnapping me?"

The elf smirks again. "I was informed that we'd have a new guest shortly, and I've been looking forward to meeting you and making your acquaintance."

"And now that you've managed that?"

The elf frowns. "The count instructed you to remain in your chambers in the main tower, did he not?"

"And what if he did?"

"You've gone against his wishes. For that, you must be punished."

You send up a silent prayer to Tyr. Before you can request a spell, though, a shadow peels itself off the wall behind Rahadin, spreads its wings, and passes through him like a ghost. You do your best to defend yourself with your torch, but the shadow demon moves right through it as well and slashes at you with its long, vicious claws. They slip through your flesh, slicing into your very being, causing you to drop your torch, which plunges the room into darkness.

While you are blinded and defenseless, the shadow demon makes quick work of you, shredding you with strike after strike from its claws. As you collapse senseless on the floor, Rahadin says, "I do hope the count's next guest won't be so rude."

THE END

When you reach the outer wall, you see that Castle Ravenloft sits atop a mountain and that there's nothing but a sheer drop on all sides. The mists below are so thick that you cannot even see the floor of the valley you assume must lie below. You consider climbing downward anyhow, hoping to find freedom.

Maybe you can manage the climb down once you reach the face of the natural cliff, but the stone walls of Ravenloft itself are slick with mist and offer little real purchase. Still, what choice do you have?

As you're about to vault over the crenellations and try your weight on some nearby vines, a voice behind you says, "You're a brave person to be sure, but that seems like certain death for you."

You spin around to find

a handsome blond-haired man with pale skin and gaunt cheeks. He offers you a false smile and a shallow bow.

"My name's Escher. Allow me to welcome you to the ranks of Count Strahd's guests."

Rather than return his bow, you shake your head. "That's not necessary. I won't be staying."

He arches a thin eyebrow at this. "You don't wish to accept Strahd's hospitality? How perfectly sensible of you."

"I don't suppose you'd be willing to show me the way out of this place?"

He rubs his chin as he sizes you up. "Actually, I would. After all, I hardly need the competition for Strahd's attention, do I? But if I'm going to do that for you, it only seems appropriate that you perform a small service for me."

You give him a suspicious glare. "What do you have in mind?"

"Strahd recently brought another guest here, a naive young thing named Gertruda. Like I said, I don't need the competition. If you'd help me to be rid of her . . ."

"I won't kill her."

Escher chuckles. "I just need you to take her with you. Doesn't that seem like the heroic thing to do?"

Maybe it would—if it didn't sound so much like a trap. Can you really trust anyone under Strahd's thrall?

Accept Escher's offer. Turn to page 69 . . .
Refuse Escher's offer. Turn to page 45 . . .

You don't quite trust the clockwork jester yet. You're willing to explore the castle—for now—but you don't like the idea of putting your fate entirely in his hands. Still, you don't like the idea of going through the door that leads to the dangerous place either. Or of winding up atop another windswept tower.

The middle door feels like the right way to go, but you just can't let Pidlwick lead the way. You push past him and open the door, not waiting for him. He rushes right after you, grumbling the entire way.

"What, don't you trust me?"

The fact that your choice puts him in a poor mood makes you feel much better about it.

A short stairwell leads up into the darkness. At the landing, you turn right, and a long hallway stretches before you. The stone here seems slick, probably due to the fog that fills the corridor from one end to the other.

Suspicious of how little you can see through the mysterious mist, even with your torch held aloft, you tread cautiously down the hallway, feeling ahead with your feet as you go. If Pidlwick wants to betray you, this would be the perfect place for it.

"What's the holdup?" Pidlwick says as he pushes past you. "There's nothing to fear down here in the depths of the castle."

"Do you get down here often?" you ask as you hesitantly follow him into the fog-shrouded darkness. Fearful that he might turn on you, you keep back a bit.

"Never," he replies with a giggle. "What would be the point?"

"Then why am I following you through here?" You stop dead in your tracks.

"What other choice do you have?" the jester asks. And then he disappears through the floor with a scream.

Through the mist, you can just see a trapdoor in the floor closing and resetting, right where Pidlwick disappeared. You don't know what happened to the creature, but you have no desire to share his fate. On the other hand, you don't want to go back either. Better the danger you already know about.

Marking off the edge of the trap, you back up several yards, then sprint forward. As you reach the mark, you take a running leap that doesn't quite clear the far side of the trap. It starts to slide open beneath you, and you land with just the upper half of your body on solid ground. You haul yourself clear.

At the end of the hallway, a door leads into the cold catacombs beneath the castle. You wander around these stone chambers and the maze they form for a long while, to no avail. Just when you're about to give up on finding your way out, you hear someone weeping.

Turn to page 68 . . .

"I think I can take it from here," you tell Pidlwick. The little jester gives you a grumpy grunt, but you ignore him. Just because you need his help doesn't mean you can trust him.

"Try going to the left," he says.

You decide to stick to the right instead.

You wade into the waters as carefully and cautiously as you can manage, feeling ahead with your feet but ready to jump back at a moment's notice. At one point, the floor beneath you starts to feel as if it's ready to give way, but you leap backward onto solid ground before anything happens. Pidlwick grunts in frustration once more. Clearly, he knew the trap was there and was hoping that you'd fall through it. You now know for sure that he can't be trusted, but you continue on your way, not wanting to tip him off that you're onto him.

Soon you emerge into a large room with a balcony high on the wall to your right, on which sit two large thrones. It overlooks a chamber filled with racks and stocks alongside rows of tools and weaponry. Chains dangle from several rings set into the ceiling, most of them terminating in manacles. Many of these are empty, but a few have bones dangling loosely inside them.

As you enter the room, the still waters begin to churn, and six slime-gray zombies push themselves up from the depths. They begin to wade toward you, their open mouths moaning in unholy hunger.

"God!" Pidlwick screams as he cowers behind you. "Run! Follow me. Run!"

You've faced undead like this before, mindless creatures brought to a hollow mockery of life by means of necromancy. And you know how to deal with them.

You raise your holy symbol before you and thrust it toward the oncoming creatures. "Back, you evil beasts!" you shout. "You're nothing before the holy power of Tyr!"

The zombies cringe away, their voices turning from moans of hunger to groans of terror.

One by one, they start to fall apart. Their groans transform into high-pitched protests for a moment before their false lives leave them forever.

An instant later, the living dead become simply the dead.

Pidlwick creeps up behind you and peers around your side. "That Tyr must really be something," he says in breathless amazement.

You look back and give the clockwork jester a proud nod. "That he is."

A quick glance around reveals no exit aside from the way you came, so, hoping to get and stay dry, you climb up one of the sets of chains and swing your way up to the railing of the balcony. Clambering over it, you take a moment to catch your breath in one of the thrones.

"What kind of rulers install thrones over a torture chamber?" you wonder aloud.

"Those who like to savor their cruelty," Pidlwick says as he lounges in the throne next to yours. "Castle Ravenloft stands as proof of what that brings."

You get up to inspect the red velvet curtains that hang behind the thrones, parting them to reveal a hidden door. Cautiously, you open it and enter a chamber beyond.

A stone brazier in the center of the room burns with a magical heatless flame. A massive hourglass hangs suspended above it, and two nine-foot-tall statues of armored knights on horseback stand in alcoves on either side of the room.

You decide to ignore all that, unwilling as you are to be drawn into one of Strahd's obvious temptations. You just want to escape.

Directly across from you, you see three doors.

Pidlwick points to the door on the right. "That just leads back up to the roof of the castle," he says. "The one on the left leads to a dangerous place. The center one is the one for you. Let me show you the way."

Pidlwick opens the door on the right to show that he's not lying. There's a spiral staircase beyond, leading up into nothing but darkness. He looks up at you with his glittering eyes.

Take the "dangerous" door. Turn to page 57 . . .

Take the door Pidlwick suggested but lead the way yourself. Turn to page 62 . . .

Trust Pidlwick and let him guide you. Turn to page 71 . . .

You follow the sound of soft weeping, trying to move as silently as you can through the countless crypts. When you reach the end of the catacombs, you find an open archway overlooking white marble steps that lead down into a high-vaulted tomb. Inside, you see a cloaked figure leaning over an intricately decorated coffin sitting atop a slab of white marble.

Even with his back to you, you recognize that the man in the tomb is Count Strahd. Peering around him, you can see a name carved into the coffin: Sergei von Zarovich. You don't know how the two men are related, but by the age of the tomb, you feel sure that Sergei has been dead for a long time.

You creep down the steps and into the tomb. Strahd doesn't seem to notice you, even with your torch burning quietly in your hand. This could be your chance to strike, to put an end to the vampire lord forever, but can you bring yourself to attack someone clearly in the throes of such tremendous grief?

Attack Strahd! Turn to page 78 . . .
Comfort Strahd. Turn to page 84 . . .

"I'll help you," you tell Escher. He claps his hands in delight. "I don't suppose I have much choice in the matter."

"Of course you don't," the man says. "But it's so refreshing to hear you acknowledge it."

Beckoning you with a crooked finger, Escher leads you back into the tower. Instead of going up or down, he moves along the landing and ducks into a darkened hallway you walked past earlier. Then he takes a sharp left and strides up to a wooden door.

Once you catch up to him, he opens the door with a flourish and ushers you into a lavish study. Bookshelves filled nearly to bursting line the room, and a roaring fire blazes in the hearth. As you walk across a plush rug, past the overstuffed chairs and couches arranged here and there, you

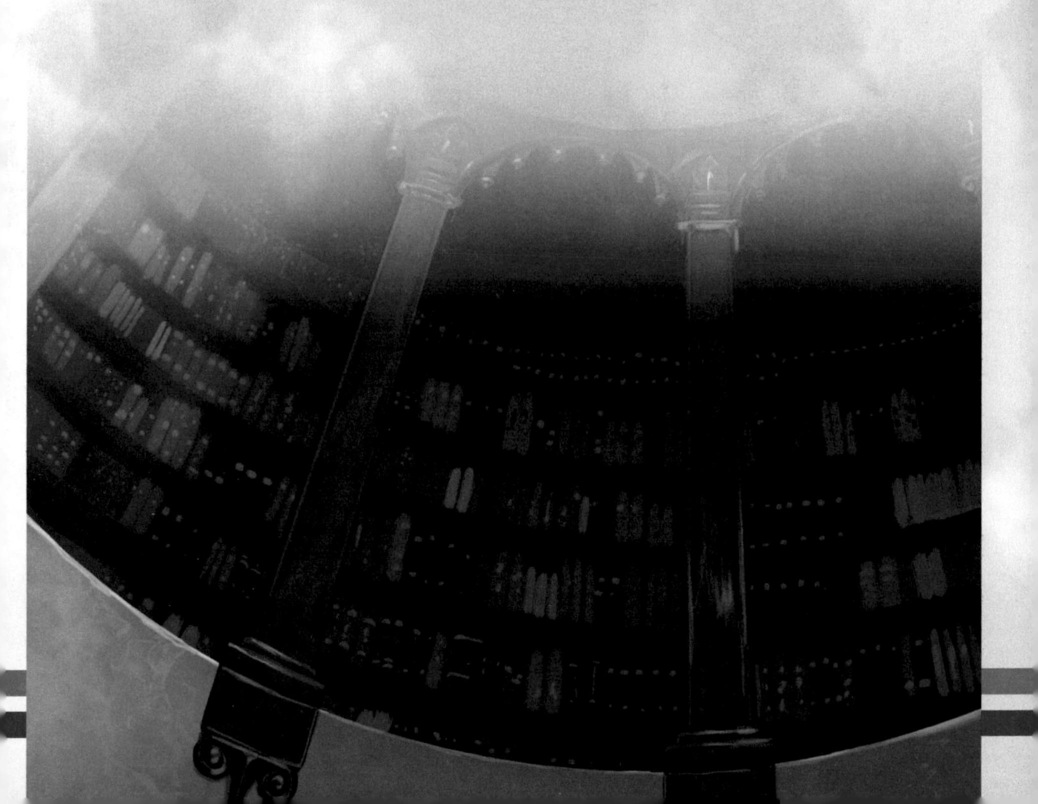

realize that this is the first room you've found in the entire castle that you'd call comfortable.

Escher moves past you and brings you to a wide pair of doors set in the opposite wall. "And here we are," he says.

The next room is the biggest bedchamber you've ever seen. Tall white candles burn throughout, and by their sweet-scented flames you can make out a massive canopied bed against the wall to the right. Straight across from you stretches a wide window, looking out over the mountainous approach to Castle Ravenloft.

A wide-eyed young woman dressed in a nightgown sits up in the bed and greets you with a dreamy smile. "Why, hello," she says. "Are you friends of Strahd?"

"We're here to rescue you," you tell her. "Get dressed, and we'll get you out of here. We don't have much time."

"Rescue me?" She laughs. "From what? A life of luxury in the company of the most sophisticated people I've ever met?"

It's then you realize that she hasn't figured out who these people are or what she's gotten herself into.

"Your life is in danger," you inform her. "As is mine, every moment we linger here."

She folds her arms across her chest. "Then you should leave. I'm staying."

Drag her with you. Turn to page 82 . . .
Leave her here. Turn to page 86 . . .

"Lead on," you tell the clockwork jester. Do you have any choice but to trust him?

He claps his metal hands with glee and then throws open the middle door. Beyond it, stairs stretch upward into the darkness, and he clambers straight up like a child on his way to a birthday party for a favorite friend.

You follow right behind him. When you reach the landing at the top of the stairs, a hallway runs off to your right. The stone corridor is damp with the mist that swirls through it, obstructing your view down the hall. Despite that, you hustle along behind the incautious Pidlwick, keeping your hand on his shoulder the entire time, just to make sure you don't lose him.

The clockwork creature leaps up and down as he prances along the hall. Just when you think you might want to let go of him, he gives a little yelp and begins to fall straight down. You snatch the back of his collar, catching him before he plunges through a trapdoor that opens in the floor before you.

The sudden change of weight almost hauls you into the pit after Pidlwick, but you manage to brace yourself just in time. Using your own weight to lever the clockwork man out of the pit, you throw yourself backward, still holding on to him. He lands on top of you in a jumbled heap, and you rest there for a moment, catching your breath.

"Thank you!" Pidlwick says. "I've no idea where that trap might have dropped me, but I can be sure it wouldn't be pleasant."

"Praise Tyr," you say as you gently move the creature off you and push yourself to your feet. You regard the floor where the trapdoor was, and you see that it's sealed itself off again.

"How are we to get across that?" Pidlwick wonders aloud, doing a hoppy little dance. "I don't think I could," he says, disappointed.

You purse your lips as you size up the creature. "I might be able to help you with that."

He cocks his head and looks up at you. "Whatever do you mean?"

Setting your torch down for a moment, you fold your hands together. As Pidlwick gives you a curious stare, you utter a short but fervent prayer to Tyr for strength. Then, before the clockwork man can object, you turn him around and grab him by the top of his pants with one hand and the back of his collar with the other.

Without ceremony, you swing him backward and then forward.

"Wait!" he cries.

You hurl him down the hall. He lands on the floor in a clatter of leather and metal—but clear of the other side of the pit.

Breathing a sigh of relief, you snatch up your torch and take several steps back, then charge right after Pidlwick. You land with one foot on the trapdoor, but you manage to drop forward and safely land on your knees next to the jester.

"See?" you say to him with a satisfied grin. "Nothing to it."

Pidlwick doesn't laugh. He stands up, brushes himself off, and starts forward again. This time there's no prancing.

Soon you find yourself in the catacombs, wandering in a maze of sealed crypts.

"I've been here before," Pidlwick says. "I came down the steps from the high tower. The place is filled with the dead, but there are three magnificent tombs here.

"The one to the north belongs to Sergei, Strahd's brother. The one to the east is that of his parents. Strahd's own tomb lies to the south."

"And which way would you go?" you ask.

"If you want to destroy Strahd, you might find him resting in his tomb. Otherwise, there's a window in his parents' tomb that might offer escape."

Go into Strahd's tomb. Turn to page 75 . . .
Enter the tomb of Strahd's parents. Turn to page 77 . . .

"I think it's time I paid Strahd a visit in his tomb," you tell Pidlwick. "That would only be courteous, don't you think?"

It's impossible to read the creature's expression as he digests your decision, but he gives you a solid nod, then pivots on his heel and takes you in what must be a southerly direction.

Pidlwick stops at an intersection in the catacombs. To the south, you can see a lowered portcullis, through which black marble steps lead down to a high-vaulted room. A thick layer of dirt covers the floor of the room, and a glossy black coffin sits in the center.

Pidlwick points at the coffin. "There it is, although he's probably not in it right now. And it's harder to get to than you think."

You spot a lever on the wall next to the tomb's entrance. "Is that for raising the portcullis?" you ask.

The jester nods, and the bells on his hat jingle. "It's getting to it that's the trick. I've never managed it. There's powerful magic here, you know."

"How do you mean?"

"You think someone as mighty as Count Strahd von Zarovich would let someone—even one of his guests—walk into his tomb?"

"What's he going to do to stop us?" you ask.

Pidlwick snickers at you and says, "Watch."

With that, he walks toward the tomb. An instant later, he disappears in a flash of blinding light, replaced by a man with rotting skin and battered armor, plus a bloodstained scimitar in his hand. He glares at you with vicious intelligence in his eyes.

"You dare despoil the count's rest? For that, you shall join me in death!"

Your mentors taught you how to deal with creatures like this. Offering up a prayer to Tyr, you thrust your holy symbol before you and command the monster to depart. "Be gone!"

To your surprise, the wight answers you with a swift swing of his sword that catches you in the side of your neck. You topple over, grasping at your wound, blood flowing through your fingers. As the wight works to finish you off, you hear a familiar sound echoing through the catacombs: Pidlwick's grating giggle.

It's the last thing you ever hear.

THE END

Pidlwick nods his assent and guides you off to the east. A wide stairwell leads down to a landing, on either side of which stands a thirty-foot-tall bronze statue of a warrior holding a spear. A soft blue curtain of light flows between the two stations, but through it you can see that the stairs go down farther to a much larger room.

"Is that a trap?" you ask, pointing at the curtain of light as the two of you walk down the stairs and stop short before it.

"Only for those impure of heart," Pidlwick says. By way of example, he proceeds into the curtain and disappears in a flash of light.

You glance around, ready for anything, and spy Pidlwick standing back at the top of the stairs, waving at you. "It doesn't hurt, but it's effective."

Giving the curtain a steely look, you say a quick prayer and walk into it. The curtain feels as if it isn't there, and it does nothing to stop you. Apparently, your heart is pure.

When you reach the bottom of the stairs, you find a gorgeously appointed tomb and see that there's one coffin set on a pedestal against the north wall and one on the south wall.

Small as he is, Pidlwick manages to worm his way around the back of one of the statues and joins you in the tomb. He points at the massive stained-glass window that occupies the eastern wall. "Magnificent, isn't it?"

Turn to page 35...

Even though he's exhibiting more emotion than you'd ever have expected from such a murderous monster, Strahd must die. As a vampire, he's an abomination who's probably murdered countless innocents—not to mention kidnapping you and imprisoning you in Castle Ravenloft. Your path here is clear.

You inspect the bottom of your torch where you snapped it off the bedpost. It's sharp enough that it might serve as a stake, and you decide to make use of it.

Creeping forward as quietly as you can, you raise your torch high over your head, ready to plunge the splintered end of it right through the vampire's back. You offer up a silent prayer to Tyr that your aim for Strahd's heart might be true.

Maybe the count hears you approach. Maybe he sees the light of the torch. Maybe he feels the heat from its flame.

Whatever it is, something gives you away a second too soon. Strahd spins around supernaturally fast, his eyes flashing red and furious.

It's probably too late, but you attack him anyhow, plunging the makeshift stake toward the vampire's chest. Strahd knocks your torch aside, sending it spinning into the darkness.

It cartwheels over the coffin, landing at the feet of a statue of a beautiful man who bears a strong resemblance to Strahd. Stone-carved angels flank the man's statue on either side. Under other circumstances, the trio might have a heavenly air about them. As it is, the lighting from your guttering torch gives them each a hellish look.

Strahd looms over you, sneering at your pathetic attempt to destroy him. "So this is how you repay my hospitality, you wretch!"

You brace yourself for Strahd's counterattack, but it never comes. Instead, he disappears, turning to a mist that briefly surrounds Sergei's coffin before vanishing.

He reappears a moment later at the top of the stairs into the crypt, where he yanks a lever. A heavy iron portcullis slams down, trapping you inside.

"Welcome to your new chambers. You can rot here alongside my damned brother!"

In the end, you do exactly that.

THE END

"All right," you tell Cyrus. "Lead on."

The twisted creature gives a little leap of glee. "Right this way," he says. "Right this way!"

He shuffles off toward the door through which you entered the hall, and you follow him. He brings you to the middle of the landing room and pulls a lever. Two portcullises slam down, trapping you there with him. The entire section of the room leaps upward, rising into the upper part of the castle at alarming speed amid the clattering of distant gears.

"What have you done?" you shout at Cyrus as you grab him.

He grins up at you and says, "The master will be pleased!"

It's then that you notice the room is filling with mist. Wait, that's not mist—it's gas!

Surprised, you break into a choking fit, trying to expel the gas from your lungs. You reach for Cyrus, but he's holding his breath and waving goodbye.

You wake sometime later, lashed to a chair in the lounge outside the room from which you escaped. Unfortunately, you're not alone. A handsome man and three gorgeous women in old-fashioned clothing stand nearby, waiting for you to wake. Once your eyes flutter open, they bare their fangs and begin to feed. . . .

THE END

You stomp over to the bed and grab Gertruda by the arm. "Ready or not, you're coming with me," you tell her. "I'm not going to leave you here to die."

Gertruda lets loose a scream so painfully earsplitting that you have to release her to protect your hearing.

"How dare you put your hands on me!" Gertruda cries. "I don't want to leave here. I've lived in the shadow of this castle my entire life, and my mother always told me how horrible and cold and terrible it was—but look at it! This is paradise, and I'm never leaving. Not with you or anyone else!"

"You're a fool!" you bark in her face. "Strahd is a vampire—a creature of incalculable evil and insatiable hunger—and you're sure to be at the top of his menu. To stay here is to condemn yourself to death!"

She pales at your words, but she's still not convinced. "You liar! You just want him for yourself."

Escher laughs out loud at this. "Well, that may be true for me," he says, putting a hand to his chest, "but this kind cleric here is only looking out for your best interests."

"You're just as bad a liar!" she says to him. "You already confessed to wanting the count all to your lonesome!"

Escher concedes to her accusation with a gentle nod. "That's because it's already too late for me," he says. "Those who succumb to Strahd's charms are forever changed by them."

"And what if that's what I want?" she says, crossing her arms over her chest. "You didn't grow up as sheltered as I did, never allowed to go outside. Now I can go anywhere—do anything—I want!"

Escher snorts at her. "Strahd may seem kind to you now, but that doesn't last long. Stay here and you'll soon wind up like my weird sisters-in-arms and me: bedding down in the cold dirt of the grave, feeding on the innocent to satisfy your unending thirst for the warm blood that no longer flows through your veins."

Turn to page 92 . . .

You clear your throat, but Strahd doesn't flinch. Does that mean he already knew you were there? Or is he simply that cold-nerved?

Clearly he heard you. There can be no doubt that he knows you are there. Perhaps he's waiting to see if you'll try to stab him in the back. Or maybe he's preparing to tear your throat out before you get the chance.

As a cleric of Tyr, you tend to focus on justice rather than death, but you've presided over more funerals than you care to count. You're regularly called upon to say something meaningful at ceremonies for the deceased and can't see why even a creature as evil as Strahd shouldn't be entitled to this courtesy.

"I'm sorry for your loss," you tell him. "Death is a natural part of the cycle of life, as much as it hurts, and grief is a key part of how we deal with those inevitable losses."

The vampire lord doesn't turn to acknowledge you, at least not at first. He remains frozen for a long moment, during which you wonder if he might spin around and gut you. But then his shoulders start to shake.

Thinking that Strahd's been overcome with emotion, you reach out and put a hand on his shoulder, offering him some quiet compassion. You stay there in silence with him, wondering if he might have something to share about his evident grief. After all, that would seem the human thing to do.

When he says nothing, you finally break the silence and ask, "Would you like me to pray with you?"

Strahd's shoulders shake harder than ever, and he starts to cough. You lean over him, trying to peer into his eyes. As you do, you realize he's not sobbing.

The vampire lord spins about, and you recoil in horror as you see how wrong you were. A huge fang-filled smile splits his deathly pale face.

"Thank you," he says with a vicious sneer. "I haven't laughed that hard since probably before your grandparents were born. The very idea that I'd need solace from someone like you over a loss centuries old . . . It's stunning."

If only you could explain yourself, but he cuts you off with a snarl.

"More than that, though, it's insulting. To think that someone like you could offer someone like me condolences . . . And then ask if I'd care to pray with you?" He shakes his head in disbelief. "Do you realize how much death I've seen? How much death I've caused?"

"My words were sincere," you tell him.

"I know." His lips curl in disgust.

Turn to page 93 . . .

Fine," you tell Gertruda. "I don't need your drama anyhow. I'm leaving now, with or without you." As Tyr teaches, you can't save those who don't want to be saved.

The young woman gives you a grim but determined look. Something insane dances in her eyes, and you wonder if perhaps you've made the wrong decision by leaving her in the count's clutches. Despite that, you turn your back on her and nod to Escher to show you the way out.

That's when the young woman grabs you by the shoulder and hauls you around to face her. "You can't fool me!" she shouts in your face. "You're going to try to steal Strahd from me!"

Stunned by the woman's ferocity, you reel backward. If she thinks you want to have anything to do with Strahd, her adoration for the count has unbalanced her.

Seeing the shock on your face, she senses her chance. She leaps at you, knocking you onto your back and landing on top of you. You don't want to hurt her, but she's not giving you much choice.

"Get off me!" you shout at her. "You're insane!"

"You claim to want to leave all this behind?" She laughs. "And you think I'm the crazy one? I don't believe you. No one's that nuts!"

Escher should be helping you, but he comes to Gertruda's aid rather than yours. He kneels behind your head and pins your arms to the floor.

"Tyr's hammer!" you shout at him. "What are you doing?"

“I started this day with two rivals for the count’s affection in the castle,” he says with a smile. “I’m happy to reduce that number by one. It doesn’t matter how.”

You struggle against them both, but Escher is supernaturally strong. He alone would probably be enough to overpower you, but with Gertruda sitting on you as well, you can barely move.

“No!” you say. “Gertruda! If you kill me, what’s to stop Strahd from killing you?”

“Kill you?” Gertruda says with genuine surprise on her face. “I’m not going to kill you. But I’m sure that once you’re unconscious, this man here will help me to eject you from the castle.”

“Although,” Escher says as he opens his mouth wide, exposing his vicious fangs, “killing him would be a lot more final.”

Gertruda’s eyes open wide at the sight of the fangs, and when Escher plunges them into your neck, she squeaks in panic and jumps to her feet. But it’s too late for you. As your vision starts to go black, you offer up one last prayer to Tyr. If there’s any justice in this world, he’ll help Gertruda to escape from this place, even though you can’t.

THE END

"It's true," you tell Rahadin, covering for Escher. "He's been trying to turn me over to Strahd ever since he found me." You hate to lie, but at the moment you care only about getting out of the castle.

Escher gives Rahadin a told-you-so smile, but the chamberlain isn't fooled for an instant. "I wouldn't take the word of either of you telling me the sun was in the sky at noon."

He looks to Escher. "I expect nothing less from you. You're a charlatan, a trickster, and a fraud, proven time and again."

He turns to you now, and your blood runs cold. "You, though, I had higher hopes for. I wish you'd proven to be a person of integrity. One I could trust in the presence of the count. As it turns out, I think there's only one thing to be done with you."

Rahadin nods, and you realize then that Escher has somehow worked his way behind you. He grabs you from behind and sinks his fangs straight into your neck. You scream in mortal agony, but it's too late to stop him. The last thing you hear is his laughter.

THE END

You step away from Escher and look at him askance. "If you think I'm going to lie for you, you're sorely mistaken."

Escher gasps as if you've stabbed him. "I never thought you'd be so bold as to lie about my intentions." He turns toward Rahadin. "I found this cleric wandering the parapets, and I decided that Count Strahd must be informed. We've been searching for him ever since, and I fully intended to toss this miscreant before him to beg for his mercy."

That makes you bark a bitter laugh. "You asked me to flee from here and to take some woman named Gertruda with me!"

"Liar!" Escher snarls. His helpful facade falls away, his handsome face contorted into vampiric ugliness. "You think you can tear me away from the count's favor? I'll have your blood for that."

You hold up your holy symbol before you, praying that Tyr's power can protect you, as foolish as you know that hope might be. Tyr may be a god, but he's a distant one, and this foul creature who wants you dead is right here.

A blade flashes before you—a curved scimitar with a sharp, glinting edge—and twists against Escher's throat. It shocks you to discover it's held in Rahadin's hand.

The chamberlain sneers at Escher. "Close your mouth and cover those fangs," he says. "If you think that I can't see through your pathetic lies, then you deserve the death I'll hand you."

"You dare draw your blade on me?" Escher growls

as he knocks the sword away with his forearm and hurls himself at Rahadin. "I'll tear the breath from your lungs!"

The chamberlain beats a measured retreat, deflecting the vampire's attacks with his blade. "Fool!" he shouts. "The master will hear of this."

The two seem like they might be occupied with each other for a while, and you don't question your good fortune. Instead, you charge straight through the doors and keep running until Castle Ravenloft is lost in the mists behind you. On your way, you offer up a well-deserved prayer of gratitude to Tyr—and another hoping that you might never see the castle or its occupants again.

THE END

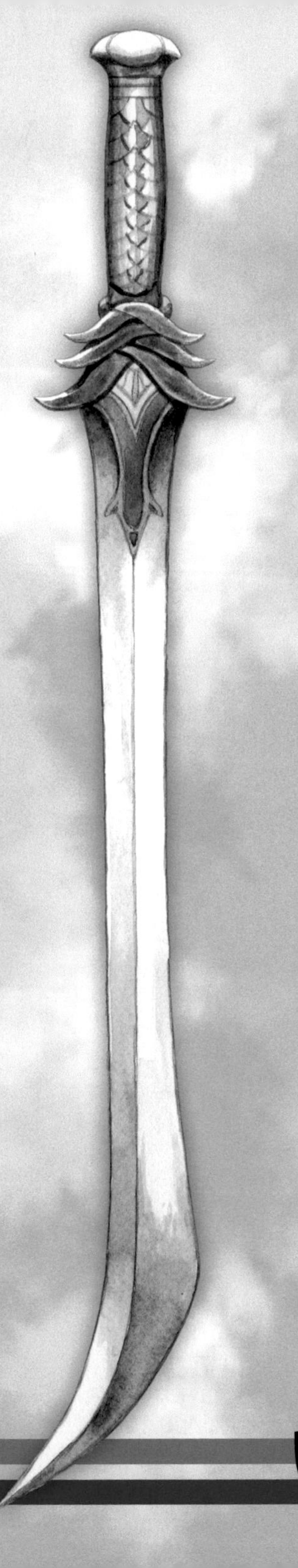

Gertruda shivers at Escher's description of life as a vampire spawn. When Escher bares his fangs at her, she shrieks and clings to your arm. "All right," she says. "You've convinced me. Why haven't we already left?"

You put yourself between Gertruda and Escher, then gesture for the vampire to lead the way. "You wanted us gone," you tell him. "Let's make that happen."

Smiling, Escher directs you to a secret door to the left of the bed. You emerge in a short hallway behind one of the many statues that line its length. From there, you take the stairs down into another secret hallway.

You cut through a vacant throne room, down a set of twinned stairs, and across the main hall to the castle's entrance. At one point, Escher motions for you to stop while he listens for something you can't hear. Once he's satisfied, he makes a mad dash for the exit and throws open the doors.

You're about to cheer, when you see that Count Strahd is outside the castle, sitting astride a horse and waiting for you.

He glares at you and says, "You're not to leave the castle. Return now, and bring Gertruda with you!"

Run for it! Turn to page 94 . . .
Pray for help! Turn to page 108 . . .
Face Strahd! Turn to page 98 . . .

Strahd gazes into your eyes and whispers a single word to you. "Sleep."

Despite struggling against his will, you find that you cannot prevail.

You wake later atop a moonlit tower of Castle Ravenloft, a chilly wind cutting through you like a hail of knives. Strahd is carrying you in his arms, his cape whipping about like a banner in the breeze. He looks down into your eyes and bares his fangs.

"Excellent," he says. "I didn't want you to miss this."

Still groggy with sleep, you realize that Strahd is standing at the edge of the tower's roof, leaning right up against the crenellations. You look down at the dizzying drop, past not only the castle itself but also the sheer cliff edge of the high plateau from which it stabs into the sky. A scream of terror erupts from your throat.

"Good," Strahd says as he hurls you over the wall. "That's exactly what I was hoping for."

You scream all the way down. As you fall, you silently pray to Tyr with all your might. Not for salvation—it's far too late for that—but for forgiveness for ever thinking you could let your guard down around such an evil beast.

THE END

Grabbing Gertruda by the arm, you take off at a dead sprint. The young woman screams in surprise but gets her feet moving just the same. She's not nearly as fast as you, but she's doing her best.

You race across the drawbridge that connects Castle Ravenloft with a narrow, winding mountain road beyond, snaking up toward you out of the surrounding mists. The drawbridge creaks as you run along it, and one of the loose boards you step on cartwheels away into the chasm below. Despite that, you make it nearly all the way to the other side before Gertruda trips and falls, sprawling across the moldering boards.

You skid to a stop and turn back to help her. As you do so, you see that Strahd hasn't followed—at least not yet. Instead, he's climbed off his horse and is taking his righteous rage at your escape out on Escher.

"How dare you betray me!" the vampire lord shouts at his spawn in unrestrained fury. "After all I've done for you? After all I've given you? So many more years of life, and you've wasted them. Spent them plotting against me!"

For his part, Escher just throws up his hands in helplessness and denies everything. "No, my count, no! I would never! I was bringing them to you. So you could give them the gift."

Strahd throws back his head and unleashes a cruel laugh. Escher falls to his knees, pleading for mercy, but the vampire lord kicks him instead, sending him sprawling across the drawbridge.

“How dare you?” Strahd says. “I decide when I bring others into my immortal fold. I decide when they’re worthy! And I don’t take recommendations from those who’ve managed to disappoint me so many times.”

Gertruda recoils from the sight of Strahd’s wrath as you help her to her feet. “To think that I ever idolized such a monster in my heart,” she says.

You wish she hadn’t said a word. That she could have just kept her mouth shut until you’d been able to get away.

Maybe you could have lost yourselves in the mists. Maybe you could have found your way back down the mountain. You might even have been able to find Gertruda’s home and hole up there with her and her mother for a while.

But for any of that to happen, Strahd would have had to remain distracted by Escher for a bit longer. Instead, his sharp ears immediately picked up Gertruda’s complaint, and he’s not pleased.

Strahd snarls in your direction, but Escher leaps up and wraps his arms around a leg of the vampire lord. “I’m so sorry, my count!” he shouts. “Please forgive me!”

Strahd yanks his leg out of Escher’s grasp. Then he picks the man up and hauls him over his head with unimaginable strength.

“No, my count!” Escher screeches. “I didn’t mean to offend you.”

Strahd barks out a bitter laugh. “Then you’ve utterly failed.”

With that, he hurls Escher off the drawbridge, and the vampire disappears, screaming into the mist-shrouded chasm.

"We need to go," you say to Gertruda. "Now."

The young woman nods at you, but she doesn't budge. You grab her by the elbow, but still she doesn't move. Her feet are frozen with fear.

"Mother was right," Gertruda whispers to herself, so low you can barely hear her. "I've been such a wicked fool."

"You can tell her all about it when you see her," you say. "But if you don't start marching out of here, you're never going to get the chance."

At that moment, Strahd points a long, thin finger in your direction. "You!"

Save Gertruda! Turn to page 100 . . .
Save yourself! Turn to page 105 . . .

You grab Gertruda and shove her behind you. "Forget it, Strahd!"

The vampire throws back his head and laughs, cold and long.

You snarl at his derision. "I don't think you understand," you tell him. "You might be able to murder us both today, but if you attempt it, I'm going to make sure that you pay dearly for it. Live or die, we're not going down without a fight."

Strahd smirks at your bravado, assuming that it's false. "You're out of your mind," he says. "I can destroy you in a dozen different ways. Do you think your defiance really counts for anything in the long run?"

"In the long run, we're all dead," you say. "Even you. And when it comes to the here and now, my defiance counts for everything. If the only pleasure I have left in this life comes from frustrating you, then I'm going to savor every blessed second of it."

Feeling Gertruda shiver behind you, you turn and see she's closed her eyes and covered her ears in an attempt to keep the vampire from taking over her mind or influencing her in any way. You're glad to see her doing something smart for once.

"I'm disappointed," Strahd says. "In both of you. I'd thought that you, cleric, could see the error in your foolish devotion to your distant god and join me. And Gertruda? I hoped to open a wider world up for her, one that she's been protected from for far too long."

"Protected from you, you mean," you tell Strahd. "If only her mother had been able to keep her from you forever, but your evil casts a long shadow across this accursed land."

Strahd fidgets in his saddle as he considers the pair of you and what your fate might be. "You realize, of course, that you can't really hurt me," the vampire lord says with a sneer. "Not in any way that means anything."

"Perhaps," you say. "A bee by itself cannot kill, it's true, but it sure can sting."

"And when the bee stings, it dies," Strahd says with a shake of his head.

"If I'm going to die anyhow, I might as well go out stinging."

Strahd tilts back his head and gives you an appraising look. "Do you really think that such a futile gesture is necessary?"

You laugh at him. "I'm the bee in this scenario. I think that call's up to me."

Turn to page 102 . . .

You're not sure if Strahd is pointing at Gertruda or you, but you decide it doesn't matter. She isn't going to be of any use against the count. The only one who has even the slightest prayer of stopping him is you.

"Go," you say to Gertruda in a low, flat voice. "Get out of here. Run while you still can."

She glances at the road snaking into the mist-shrouded distance, and she shudders in fear. "But there's no way—"

You cut her off. "It's your only chance. I'll hold him off for as long as I can. Go! Now!"

She flinches at your words, stepping backward. She opens her mouth to protest, but when she sees Strahd calmly climb back on his horse and slowly walk along the drawbridge toward you as if he doesn't have a worry in the world, she claps a hand over her mouth instead. Then she turns on her heel and sprints off down the road.

Before the mists can envelop her, you turn back toward Strahd. He keeps his eyes fixed on you, not even giving Gertruda a glance. You realize a part of you had hoped that he might chase her rather than confronting you, but it seems he's fine with you making that decision for him.

So be it.

"Come and get me, Strahd!" you shout at him. "You think it's okay to kidnap people in the middle of the night and make them your prisoners? By Tyr's hammer, I have something to say about that!"

Strahd laughs at your bravado, entirely unimpressed. Then he throws his arms wide, his long-nailed fingers curled toward the cloud-shrouded moon above.

"You think you can talk me into letting you go? You think your god will answer your prayers? You think you have any chance of leaving my castle alive?"

You chuckle at him, trying not to let him see you shiver. "I've already managed to escape from your castle, haven't I? What more can you possibly have to throw at me?"

Almost instantly you regret your bravado, as Strahd's face splits into a smile only ever seen in nightmares.

"You really want to test me, cleric?" He sneers. "You'll soon realize your foolishness."

His words send a cold shiver racing through your body, and you swallow heavily.

Turn to page 113 . . .

Strahd laughs and flashes what you're sure he thinks of as a winning smile, despite his vicious fangs.

"I like your spirit!" he says. "That's exactly why I picked you out of that crowd of cattle in Daggerford and brought you back here to my castle. I don't want to kill you. I still want to recruit you."

Your jaw drops. After everything you've done to escape the castle, Strahd still thinks there's a chance you'd want to work for him? "That's ridiculous!" you say.

"Is it?" He arches a thin eyebrow at you. "Your distant god might give you some crumbs from his table, but imagine the power I can give you directly. I could use someone with your determination and wisdom. You would be my chief lieutenant throughout Barovia. No one could stand before you."

From anyone else, such an offer would be tempting, but from a vampire? You grind your teeth as you consider your options. "And if I refuse?" you ask.

Strahd gives you a casual shrug of his shoulders. "Then you shall die. And really, what a waste that would be."

Accept Strahd's offer. Turn to page 118 . . .

Refuse! Turn to page 121 . . .

As Strahd speaks, a ray of sunlight rises above the mountainous horizon and breaks through the clouds at the edge of the sky, shining down on the bridge all around you. The clouds were so thick that you hadn't even noticed that daylight might be coming.

Strahd hisses at the beam of light and throws his cloak up over his face for a moment, seemingly fearful that the sun could actually burn him. The ray doesn't quite reach far enough to do that, though, leaving him unharmed.

"Your god might be able to protect you," Strahd says with a determined sneer as he realizes he's safe, "but you're still mine."

With that, he points at you and curls his finger. You feel him trying to worm his way into your mind, and you fight off his influence with a grateful prayer to Tyr. Gertruda, though, isn't so lucky.

Before you can stop her, she lurches to her feet, out of the spot of sunlight, and begins walking toward the count. From the way she shuffles along, you know he must have mesmerized her, making her will his own.

Leave Gertruda to her fate! Turn to page 116 . . .
Save Gertruda! Turn to page 110 . . .

You and Gertruda look at each other, neither of you quite sure which of you Count Strahd is pointing at. It strikes you then that there's a solution to this particular problem. All you need to do is make the vampire choose between the two of you.

"We need to split up!" you tell Gertruda as you push her down the road. "You run for your home. I'll take to the mountains."

She clings to your arm, terrified. "No!" she screams. "You can't leave me with him. He'll chase me down on the road and kill me like a dog."

The vampire calmly climbs back onto his horse, which then takes slow, purposeful steps across the drawbridge, growing closer to you every second. Strahd is in no hurry, though. In fact, he's enjoying this.

Under other circumstances, you'd like to turn and charge him. To take him down and send him back to his grave. To snuff out the unlife animating him so he can rot the way he should have centuries ago.

Maybe if you had your armor and your weapons. If you had some friends by your side. If you had more than just your faith in Tyr.

But you already know how well that's worked for you so far. Standing up to Strahd means certain doom.

It comes down, then, to either you or Gertruda. Maybe if you force Strahd to choose between you, one of you can get away. Maybe you don't both have to die. At least not today.

You tell yourself that you're doing this for the greater good. That you don't secretly hope that Strahd will go after Gertruda instead of you. But you have a hard time making yourself believe it.

Despite that, you shove Gertruda away. "Then go into the mountains," you tell her. "I'll take the road."

She shakes her head, tears of sheer terror streaming down her face. "I'd never make it in the mountains alone. You have to take me with you. You have to save me. Please!"

In her mind, she has good reason to be scared, and she's probably right. Without you to help her, she might simply perish in the mountains. She's likely to die either way.

But that doesn't mean you should have to die with her, right? Where, you ask Tyr, is the justice in that?

Strahd throws back his head and laughs at your torment. You know that if you don't move now—at this very moment—you're dooming both of you for sure.

Shaking Gertruda off, you dash into the woods off the side of the road. The brush there is thick, obscuring your view of the drawbridge almost immediately, but that's exactly what you want. You glance back at the road just before it's entirely out of sight, and you see Gertruda standing there, staring after you in shock.

"Run, you fool!" you shout at her.

Then you're gone, shoving your way through the undergrowth, searching for somewhere to go, anywhere to hide. In the distance, you hear the howling of wolves, and you wonder if they're inside Castle Ravenloft or roaming much closer to you. You decide it doesn't matter. You need to keep running either way.

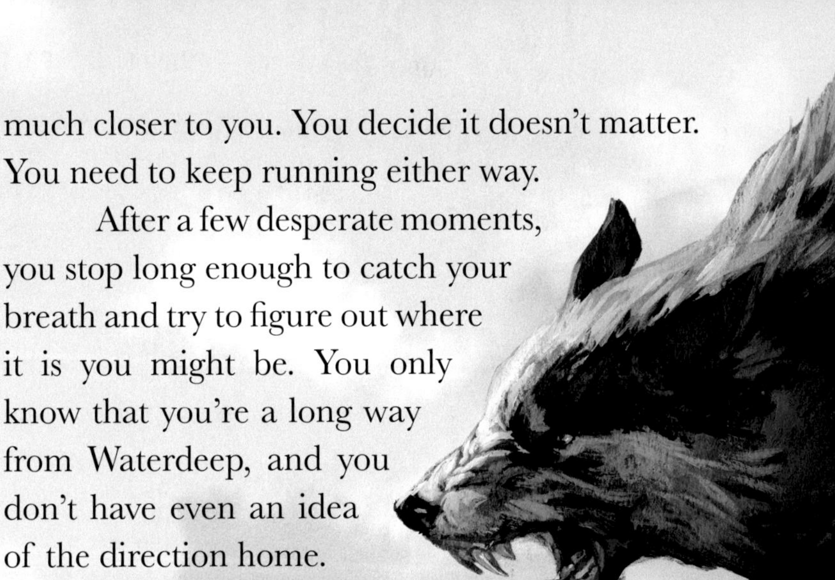

After a few desperate moments, you stop long enough to catch your breath and try to figure out where it is you might be. You only know that you're a long way from Waterdeep, and you don't have even an idea of the direction home.

At that instant, Gertruda's scream pierces the night like a needle through a funeral shroud: sharp and undeniable. You curse Strahd and the horrible choice he forced upon you, but you promise yourself as you slink off into the forest that you'll come back someday—for justice.

THE END

You realize that Strahd has you right where he wants you. Returning to Castle Ravenloft with him would only mean putting off death for a bit longer. Running from him—or fighting him—could only mean it happens right now. This is as rotten a choice as you've ever had to face.

You'd prefer to run, but it doesn't seem realistic. On foot, you have no chance of outrunning a vampire on his horse. And if—well, when—he catches up with you, you have no way to defend both yourself and Gertruda. At least no earthly way.

"You don't need them," Escher says to Strahd as he steps up next to his master's horse. "You already have the ladies in your crypt to keep you company. And you have me."

Strahd is unimpressed by Escher's observation. "That's exactly why I want the cleric at my side. I need someone far more competent than you. Someone who can actually get things done rather than lounge around the castle all night."

"I can do that for you," Escher implores as he reaches to grab Strahd by the leg and beg. "Just give me a chance instead of them! Please, my count!"

Disgusted, Strahd reaches down and smacks Escher to the ground with a backhand to the cheek. You can see that the vampire lord is likely to leap off his horse and murder him next. You're not sure that would be a loss you'd normally mourn, but Escher did get you this far. On top of that, if Strahd becomes furious enough to kill someone close to him, you and Gertruda are sure to be next.

As Strahd reaches for Escher, you fall down on your knees, fold your hands before you, and begin praying at the top of your lungs. "Hear me, O Tyr!" you call out. "Save your faithful servant from the horrors of this night. Carry me away from this monster who rules over Castle Ravenloft! Redeem me from his terrible crimes."

Strahd turns to stare at you. He doesn't say a word. He just glares at you as you pray.

Seeing his chance, Escher worms his way over the edge of the drawbridge and disappears underneath it, clinging to it like a spider. Strahd doesn't seem to notice, although you suppose he knows where Escher lays his head. He can always find him later.

"O Tyr!" you continue as you reach out and guide Gertruda down to kneel beside you. "If I have somehow offended you, please forgive me. But even if that cannot be so, please don't forsake my sister here, for she's innocent of any crime but innocence itself. Don't let her suffer at the hands of this foul beast. I beseech you!"

"Foul beast?" Strahd says with a sniff as he urges his horse closer to you. "There's no need to be insulting."

Turn to page 103 . . .

You cannot let someone as innocent as Gertruda fall into the clutches of Strahd, no matter how misguided she might be. "Don't be a fool!" you call after her. Maybe she hears you, but if she does, your words don't even cause a stumble in her step.

If only you'd held on to her rather than letting her walk free. You step forward to go after her, but as you do, you move from the warmth of the sunbeam and into the chill that seems to permeate all of Barovia. The light that Tyr sent to protect you doesn't follow you as you go.

Tyr clearly sent the sunbeam to save you, as there was no justice in your being murdered by the vampire lord. As a cleric of Tyr, you've led a good and faithful life, hewing to your calling and handing out justice wherever you could. If you voluntarily forsake Tyr's mercy, though, it seems that he's not going to argue with that. He'll simply let you suffer the consequences of your terrible decision.

Despite that, you just cannot bring yourself to abandon Gertruda to Count Strahd's nonexistent mercies. Where is the justice in letting a foolish but innocent young woman become mesmerized by a vampire and walk off to her death? Whether Tyr will offer you protection or not, you must go after her.

You make a mad dash toward Gertruda before the vampire lord can claim her as his own. Grabbing her, you spin her around, but she looks at you with blank eyes, confused as to what's happening. It's almost as if she's sleepwalking.

"You need to come with me," you tell her.

She resists you, but she's not that strong, and her heart's not in the fight. You manage to haul her back into the sunbeam, where you throw her on the ground and sit on her to keep her from squirming away. She halfheartedly tries to shove you off.

"But I want to go back to the castle," she says in a distant voice. "I want to be with Strahd."

"This is for your own good," you tell her. You look up at Strahd and see that he's laughing at you.

"You really think your sunbeam will stop me?" he says, amused. "I have living minions I can send to attack you, and they'd think the sunlight the greatest pleasure of their day. Moreover, I'm immortal. I have nothing but time. At the very least, I can remain here and wait for the sun to set again." He looks down at Gertruda trying to worm away from you. "Can you?"

You want to scream. Instead, you haul Gertruda to her feet and prepare to try to drag her down the mountain with you.

Turn to page 119 . . .

You look high up over Strahd's outflung arms and see four long, sinuous shadows cross over the face of the cloud-cloaked moon. The count laughs as they spread their leathery wings. They seem almost like gigantic bats for a moment, but they're too long, too fast.

They turn toward you, and you realize that your holy symbol isn't going to do you any good. One of the creatures dives for you, slashing past you with its claw-tipped wings, creating a wind that blows you from your feet.

You catch a glimpse of it as it passes, and then of the next as it slashes at you with its tail, drawing blood from your face and a cry from your lips.

Fangs. Claws. Scales.

Red scales and flashes of fire from their jaws.

These aren't bats. They're young dragons.

Perhaps you could have prevailed against one of them, but not four. Especially not with Strahd on their side.

Despite that, you shove yourself to your feet, and, seeing nothing else for it, you charge straight at the vampire lord, bellowing in righteous fury the entire way.

You never reach him. The wyrmlings see to that.

At least Gertruda got away.

THE END

Strahd's eyes flare bright red, and for a moment you think that the deal is off. That he'll kill you both right then and there, just to prove that no one ever gets to tell him what to do with the souls trapped within his land.

Instead, he climbs off his horse and strolls up to Gertruda, who stares up at his cruel face, her wide eyes damp and her small frame shivering. She remains stock-still, frozen in fear, as he reaches out and holds her by the chin with his pale fingers.

"Is this what you want, child?" he asks her. "As I recall, you came to my doorstep on your own and presented yourself to impose upon my hospitality, which I gave you freely. Do you now wish to abandon Castle Ravenloft for the humble home in which your mother kept you cloistered for so many years?"

Gertruda swallows hard, apparently too scared to speak. Then she gives him a firm nod. "Yes, please," she whispers, her voice breaking with fear.

Strahd frowns. His upper lip curls, and you wonder if he might snap Gertruda's neck right then and there. Instead, he drops his hand from the young woman and takes a step back to face you.

"As a show of good faith, I'll release Gertruda from my care." He gives you a meaningful look. "Will that do?"

You turn to Gertruda with a grim smile. "Run," you tell her. "Run, and don't look back."

Gertruda opens her mouth, and you worry that she might object to your deal and ruin it all. Instead, she just whispers, "Thank you." Then she turns and runs.

The mists swallow her entirely as you and Strahd watch her go.

Escher emerges from wherever he'd been hiding and stands beside you, looking disturbed at how everything has turned out. You turn to Strahd.

"I'm ready," you say, conceding your life to him. "Does becoming a vampire hurt?"

"Only the dying part," he says. "But in time you'll come to miss even that."

THE END

Gertruda!" you shout in one last attempt to save the young woman as she walks away from you and toward Strahd's embrace. "Come back!"

You could chase after her, but then Strahd would have you both, and that seems like a foolish way to waste a god's intervention. You already know what you have to do, but your feet are rooted to the spot, and you can't take your eyes off the scene unfolding in front of you.

"Don't bother," Strahd says as he reaches forward and takes Gertruda by the hand. She doesn't resist. "She's mine."

The count glares at you as he turns Gertruda around so you can see her face. Her eyes are glassy and bright. If she's not showing any fear of the count, it's because she can't feel anything at all. She is a mere puppet in his grasp.

The vampire sneers at you. "Be thankful that I'm satisfied with her for now. If I were you, I would take this opportunity to flee while you still can."

He doesn't need to tell you twice. As much as the guilt already sits badly in your stomach, you turn and run. As you charge down the rutted road that leads away from Castle Ravenloft, the sunbeam follows you, offering Tyr's protection as you retreat.

When you reach the first bend in the road, you see a horse and carriage that seem to have been abandoned. You trust that this is another sign of your god's favor and leap up, taking the horse's reins. With one good crack, the horse launches itself forward at a fast trot. Soon the carriage is rolling down the mountain at breakneck speed.

It isn't until you near the edge of the forest that you dare to look back. The castle is all but hidden from view, but it is as though you can feel the eyes of its inhabitants on you, even from this distance, and you wonder whether this will be the last you see of them. A shiver runs down your spine, and with another crack of the reins, you put the forest behind you.

THE END

You don't see that Strahd has given you much choice. It's either his way or the grave—and you're not quite ready to give up on breathing yet. Still, you cannot just give in to him like that.

"All right," you say, "let's say I'm considering your offer. What kind of authority would you grant me?"

Strahd purses his pale lips and looks pleasantly surprised. "You'd be in command of all my forces outside of Castle Ravenloft, and you'd have a home within my halls for eternity."

Gertruda whimpers behind you. If you join Strahd, she's likely doomed—unless you can do something to prevent that.

"What about the other people in Barovia?" you ask the vampire lord. "Would they be under my power as well?"

"Insofar as your wishes fall in line with my own," he says, suddenly suspicious. "In this land, my word is law."

You cannot help but nod your acceptance of that fact. "Then I'll join you, of my own free will, if you grant me one favor."

"Which is?"

You pull Gertruda to your side, and she lowers her hands from her ears, her eyes wide with terror. "You'll spare the life of this woman."

Turn to page 114 . . .

You swing Gertruda around and throw her over your shoulder. She protests just enough to make everything awkward, but she's too weak to fight you.

When you start running down the road from Castle Ravenloft, the sunbeam moves with you. You feared that Tyr would think he'd done enough to help you already, but it seems you're still in his favor.

With the sun on your back, you run as fast as you can. Only a hundred yards from the drawbridge, though, the thunder of a horse's hooves overtakes you. The beast charges into you and knocks you sprawling. Gertruda tumbles down the road, and Strahd races past you to scoop her up.

You lie there in the thinning sunbeam, shivering despite its warmth.

"Defy me again, and I'll slay you where you stand," Strahd says as he rides off with Gertruda slung over the back of his horse. "Be gone from my realm forever!"

That seems perfectly reasonable to you. As Strahd disappears into Castle Ravenloft, you start back down the road.

THE END

You're the epitome of evil," you say to Strahd. "And I could never work for you. May Tyr give me the strength to strike you down instead."

Strahd gives you a sad shake of his head. "Do you really think that could possibly happen? Better people than you have tried to finish me. They've come fully armed and armored with entire armies at their backs." He peers past you at Gertruda. "And they claimed far more powerful allies than a girl in a nightgown." He casts back his cloak and throws his arms wide open. "And yet here I am."

You step toward Strahd, still defiant. "You may well murder me here—an innocent who never even knew about you until today, nor wished you any harm—but you'll not break me. My faith in Tyr and in the cause of justice shall not be shattered, no matter what you do to me."

Strahd allows himself a disappointed chuckle. "Much as I had hoped you'd be wise enough to accept my offer, I suppose I never really believed you would. I lose so many wonderful guests this way that you'd think I'd give up on the notion. Yet I keep on trying. I suppose that's what you do when eternity stretches out before you. If I didn't believe that the odds would eventually turn in my favor, I'd have given up long ago. Despite that, I don't have the luxury of surrendering to fate. I must always forge my own destiny."

You march toward the vampire lord, your jaw jutting out in defiance. "If you're going to kill me, can you do it now? Before you bore me to death with your self-indulgent rationalizations?"

Strahd puts a hand to his chest and lances you with a mocking glance. "You wound me."

"Don't I wish that I could," you say, relishing the thought. You know that you're doomed, though. You probably were from the moment you woke in Castle Ravenloft, alone, unarmed, and without anyone but Tyr by your side.

It's hard to blame Tyr for that, though. As you know from his teachings, justice isn't something that just happens naturally in the world, all on its own. It's something that only good people can create together in an effort to bring some fairness into unfair lives.

Despite all your efforts to make yours a more just existence, you wonder if your god will welcome you into the afterlife. You did your level best to live a good and true life, full of purpose. Maybe you failed to balance the scales while you were still breathing, but you pray that you can manage it in death.

You're about to find out.

THE END

The images in this book were created by Adam Paquette, Autumn Rain Turkel, Ben Oliver, Brynn Metheney, Chris Seaman, Claudio Pozas, Conceptopolis, Daarken, Eric Belisle, Jedd Chevrier, Jesper Ejsing, Kieran Yanner, Lake Hurwitz, Lars Grant-West, Mark Behm, Milivoj Ćeran, Richard Whitters, Sidharth Chaturvedi, Vincent Dutrait, Vincent Proce, Wayne England, Zack Stella, and Zoltan Boros.

The cover illustrations were created by Eric Belisle, Mark Behm, and Ben Oliver.

Written by Matt Forbeck
Designed by Wendy Bartlett
Edited by Kirsty Walters
Published in the U.K. 2019 by Studio Press Books,
part of Bonnier Books U.K.

First U.S. edition 2019
Library of Congress Catalog Card Number 2019938947
ISBN 978-1-5362-0922-8 (hardcover) 978-1-5362-0923-5 (paperback)
19 20 21 22 23 24 WKT 10 9 8 7 6 5 4 3 2 1
Printed in Shenzhen, Guangdong, China
Candlewick Press, 99 Dover Street, Somerville, Massachusetts 02144
visit us at www.candlewick.com

Don't miss the other Dungeons & Dragons®
Endless Quest® titles!

Escape the Underdark
Into the Jungle
To Catch a Thief
Big Trouble
The Mad Mage's Academy

Or these Dungeons & Dragons titles available from
Candlewick Press:

Monsters and Heroes of the Realms
Dungeonology